Grace Found Me

SHAIDA ESCOFFERY

DEDICATION

To anyone struggling to forgive, to anyone faced with abuse, and low self-esteem. His grace is sufficient.

CONTENTS

ACKNOWLEDGMENTS

I can't believe it's been over ten years since I wrote this story. This was my first book ever! Thank you so much to my friends and family that really encouraged me and nurtured my love of writing, even at such a young age!

1 THE KNOT

"Please, I need this job!"

"How old are you anyway?" The owner of the restaurant stared me down. "Look, go home, kid."

I felt my anger rising, he wasn't listening. "That's not an option!"

Oh no, I was never going to get the job now.

"Look, I'm sorry, but I just really need this job." I searched his honey colored eyes for a speck of hope.

"You start tomorrow at 10:00. Black pants, black shirt. Don't even think about being late."

And there it was. I felt relief wash over me.

"Thank you so much." I exited the building nearly doing a little dance or screaming until my lungs collapsed, in my entire eighteen-year life span I had never been given the opportunity to achieve on my own, except for the grades that kept my mother sufficiently content. Everything had always gone according to plan, both of us had gotten what we wanted in the end; she, her riches. And me, my freedom. I had gotten away. *Check*. I now had a job. *Check*. I just had to find somewhere to live. Easier said than done, I had no money. Continuing to walk down the street, I got to the address Kelly had given me. She was an old friend who I'd told about my stepfather. We could empathize with each other. Our freshman year of high school she had gotten raped at a party. No one believed her, not even her parents, because she had a reputation as a "slut". I believed her.

She was the only one I could think of turning to without becoming homeless. She was one year older than me, yet she was living in Manhattan. Her parents were probably still footing her bills. Swirls of cold air blew all around me while I stood mesmerized by the sign and paralyzed by the difficult road ahead. I began to remember.

"Sweetheart, I'm going to go for a fitting." I heard my mother. I ran to the bathroom, locking away what I knew was eminent. His footsteps clunked throughout the house. I shivered because I could already feel his icy cold grip. He wasn't human, he couldn't be, humans had mercy and compassion, humans don't do this. Loud raps on the door filled the air.

Don't answer. Don't even make a peep. Maybe he'll go away.

A key went through the door and fear gripped my heart. His steely gaze was suddenly on me as I cowered in the corner.

"Were you trying to run away?"

Don't answer. Don't even make a peep. Maybe he'll go away.

"You shouldn't. I'm not a bad guy, Naomi; I just want to show how much I love you." His hands were on me now. "How much I love being your new daddy."

Love shouldn't feel like this, it shouldn't. This wasn't how it looked on TV.

No, non, nein, Iie, Bu shi, nao.

No one heard me, as my body grew rigid, and the knots in my stomach tightened just a little more.

I buzzed in for her.

A muffled voice came over the intercom. "Hello."

"Hey, Kelly, it's Naomi."

"Oh, hey, I'll come down and meet you."

I bounced up and down outside trying to stay warm until I saw her coming through the glass on the door. She opened up and gave me a tight hug. Kelly had always been beautiful to me with her long, curly, dark hair. Her parents had been immigrants from Puerto Rico, her father was a dentist and her mother a lawyer who both wanted her to become a professional. From the time I had known Kelly, she'd never known what she wanted to do with her life, one minute it was hairdressing, the next it was acting, singing, or simply being a basketball wife.

"It's been so long!"

"I know."

"Come on, let's got out of the cold," she said ushering me inside. I followed her as she walked towards he apartment.

"This is a nice building," I said as we walked on the gleaming wooden floors.

"Thanks. It better be nice, the amount of money it costs to live here is ridiculous." We got to her door and she pushed her key in the lock, opening the door. The apartment was beautiful, with the same wooden floors and her clean color scheme of white and grey.

"You brought a lot a clothes," she said, heading to the fridge. "Do you want something to drink?"

"Water, please," I said taking off my boots, scarf, and gloves. I moved to the couch and sat while she brought me water and sat down next to me.

"Did you get out without them noticing?" she asked.

"They were out," I said. "Viv noticed, but I wouldn't tell her where I was going."

"She didn't try to stop you?"

"No. She gave me a headstart." Viv was the only one in that house that I would remotely miss.

Kelly opened her mouth to say something before stopping herself. "Well, it's good to start over."

I sighed. "Yes, it is. I got a job waitressing today. I can't believe how lucky I got. I just walked in and begged. I'm still in shock that it worked."

"What restaurant?"

"Riveria. It's about ten blocks down."

"That's great!"

"Yes, so I can get some money together and be out of your hair as soon as possible."

"Naomi, you're welcome to stay you know."

"Thanks, but you know that I don't like being a bother."

Sunlight. I opened my eyes, taking in the unfamiliarity of my new room. I yawned and stretched before getting out of bed and heading to the bathroom to shower and brush my teeth. When I finished getting ready for work I headed out into the kitchen. Kelly peeked out from her room. "Getting ready for work?" he asked.

"Yep."

"Feel free to eat anything." She came out and sat down on a barstool.

"Thanks," I said, opening the fridge. I spotted some eggs and took them out. "Are you heading out to school today."

"No...I'm actually not in school anymore."

"Oh...I didn't know." I said, looking around for a frying pan.

"Bottom cabinet," she said. "Yeah, we both know school was never for me. Come on, I'm pretty sure they only let me in the school cause my dad and mom made some generous donation anyway."

"So, what are you gonna do?" I asked.

"Well, I didn't tell you this before, but I'm sorta dating a basketball player someone right now."

"You are?"

"Yeah. It's been awesome, I get to travel, I get to stay in this apartment."

"Wait, he pays for this?"

"Yeah. I couldn't afford this on my own. When my parents realized that I dropped out of school, they cut me off."

"Is he ok with me being here?"

"Yeah, he'll be fine."

"Are you sure?" I said hesitantly.

"Naomi, it's my apartment too. I can invite whoever I want. It's not like you're some guy."

"Ok," I said, even though it still didn't feel ok.

"You have twenty minutes to get to work. You better get going."

"Yeah, I should," I said pulling on my coat. "Wish me luck," I said as I left.

I turned on the Maps app on my phone because clearly I had no sense of direction to remember the route I'd just walked yesterday. I was power walking and continually dodging pedestrians all the while The Brandenburg Concerto. By 9:52 I had gotten to the restaurant and already my feet were hurting with my knee-high boots.

I pushed the door open, Sam, my employer, was standing there. "Hey I'm here."

"Yep, and on time, too. I was just getting ready to fire you."

This was going to be hard.

"Okay, this is Lisa; she'll show you the ropes."

Lisa was a pretty brunette with apple green eyes. Her smile was radiant; she almost looked perfect, like a model.

"Sam's gonna make you a waitress tonight." She said quickly as her body language commanded that I followed her.

Panic flooded my veins. "He's trying to see if you've got what it takes. Don't get nervous. When a customer sits down, you take their order, don't even think about writing it out fully; make abbreviations. After you take the order, put it in the touch screen computer over there," She pointed in the direction of a flat screen computer. "Make sure you get the order right and put on a sweet face because sometimes the people that come in here have money and they'll let you know that you're wasting it," She smiled, warming the mood. "Don't be scared. I started this job two years ago when I was nineteen and I'm still here. Sam's not that bad," She leaned in close, "Besides I think he likes you, he says you got spunk."

I smiled, at least he liked me. A lean college student in a NYU sweater walked in the door and sat at a table.

"Okay, there's your queue." She handed me a menu, a notepad, and a pen.

I walked up to him, my legs feeling like lead and my throat drying.

"Hi, can I take your order?" I said sweetly, making sure to smile.

"Just a coffee, and a cinnamon bun," He hardly even looked at me.

"Okay, coming right up." I went to the computer and put the order in. This was easier than I thought. Sam was a pretty good chef because in five minutes I was able to give Mr. NYU his order. This was easier than I thought. Wrong. The crowd picked up at about 12:00, lunch hour. I had four to five tables to handle at one time and I made a horrible decision to wear heels to work. By the end of my shift at 6:00, I was exhausted.

Sam called me over. Oh no. "Hey, good job today kid." My heart jumped. "So tomorrow, same time."

"Yes."

Exiting Riviera, my place of employment, I had to admit I liked the sound of that; I hummed a tune, one I invented myself. I remembered my violin that I had left in my suitcase. I hadn't played even once in two whole days. The trip back to Kelly's apartment seemed faster than the walk this morning. I used the key Kelly had given me and went inside. As soon as I entered the apartment I saw Kelly on the couch looking at me with anticipation.

"So how did it go?"

"Great, my boss said I did a good job."

"That's good. Your day sounds more interesting than mine. All I did was watch TV and take some pictures for Instagram."

I laughed. "Do you make any money from being insta-famous?"

"Yeah, I make some money."

"Well, then if anyone asks, tell them you worked from home today," I said, giving her a wink. I headed to my room and got my violin case. I pulled my violin out.

"I'm glad you still play, you were always so good."

"Thanks," I said preparing my violin. "Any song requests?"

"Just play anything that comes to your mind." Kelly rose up on her elbows on the arm of the couch, looking like a little kid anticipating a bedtime story.

I began to play and my heart felt as heavy as marble. The beginning notes played a sad tune, then suddenly the notes rose higher on the G clef and my tune grew faster and faster and my head was spinning. I played furiously as if I was blaming the violin for my troubles, as if it was the source of my misery. No, it wasn't it was the only thing that saved me from this. It took me away, it made me forget, and my tune got lighter. My head reached equilibrium and I ended my song. I looked up at Kelly, exasperated. Her eyes looked glassy.

"Oh my gosh, I never knew someone could play like that."

I felt a little embarrassed and Kelly said, "Naomi, you played from your heart."

I sat down on the barstool and stared upward, fully spent from working today.

"Do you still play the piano?" she asked.

"I haven't played in awhile," I answered dully.

"You should keep playing."

I nodded. "I'm tired, I think I'm going to turn in early," I said before I walked off to my room.

I pulled out my headphones as the homeless woman close by the Riveria spoke to me. She had a brown face weathered by age and drug use. But her eyes were kind as she smiled at me.

"I'm sorry, I didn't hear you," I said.

"I was asking if you had any spare change, so I can get something to eat."

I had just spent the money I had earned in tips on groceries and a new Metro Card. "I'm so sorry, I don't have any money but if you're hungry I can get you something to eat and bring it right out for you."

"You can?"

"Yes, ma'am, I work at the restaurant right there," I said pointing to the Riveria.

"Nice to see a pretty girl like you employed and doing something with herself."

"Thank you."

"You in school?"

"No, ma'am."

"You should be. I can bet you're smart."

"I'd like to think so," I said. "Let me get that food for you Ms..." I said wanting to change the subject.

"Ramona."

"Ms. Ramona, I'll be back."

I walked over to the Riveria. "Good morning," I said as I greeted everyone. "Where's Sam?" I asked Lisa.

"He's in the kitchen."

"Thanks," I said, heading over there and seeing sam doing some food prep. "Hey Sam, I have a favor to ask."

"What is it?"

"There's a homeless lady and I kinda promised her something to eat. Is there something we can give her?"

"We?" he said. "Don't you mean, 'you'?"

"Yes, Sam, just anything you can whip up. I'll pay you back through my tips at the end of the day."

"Fine," he said grumpy.

I walked away and started preparing for the day and waiting for Sam to finish. He came and brought out a brown bag.

"It's some scrambled eggs, bacon, fruit and two croissants. I threw a water bottle in there too."

"Merci, Sam," I said taking the bag and heading outside.

"That's gonna be $6.50," he yelled as I headed out the door.

"Yeah, I got it."

I walked down the street and found Ramona still sitting there. "Here you go. Nice and warm."

"Oh, I didn't think you'd really come back."

"But, I said I would."

"Oh, people always say that, and they never come back." I stared at her and nodded my head in understanding. I took a deep breath. "My name is Naomi, and I promise every morning and every evening I will bring you something to eat. Just between me and you."

"You don't have to promise me that."

"I want to." I touched her hand. "You can hold me to it. Every morning and every evening."

Her hand was shaking, and her eyes were glassy. "Thank you," she whispered.

"Have you gone to any shelters?"

She laughed. "I'd rather be out here than in one of them shelters. You get jumped and people steal your stuff."

"I'm sorry, I didn't know."

She didn't call me a naïve child, but it was like I could read it in her eyes. Her understanding that we were two people from vastly different worlds. She only nodded and opened the bag and pulled out a croissant. "You should head on into work. Wouldn't want you to get fired, Naomi."

I smiled. "See you for dinner, Ms. Ramona."

"You don't have to call me Ms." she said. "Ramona is just fine with me."

"Ok, Ramona. I'll see you later."

"See you later, Naomi."

It's been a week since I've been bringing Ramona food. I've started to budget for it. I've also brought her a bag full of toiletries. She hasn't stopped thanking me and I haven't stopped hoping that each day she will be safe.

"You go to church Naomi?"

Church? I haven't been to a church in years. We only popped in an out when I was younger. I don't believe that God exists. Why would a good God allow so much evil in the world? Why would he allow evil to marry my mother?

"No, I don't."

"I just thought you did, because it's usually those Christian folks that do these kinds of things for people like me."

"You don't have to be a Christian to do nice things for people, I know plenty of 'Christian' people who are mean."

She didn't say anything, she only smiled faintly. "There was a woman who used to come by and help me. We used to work together. Her name was Lorna. She was a Christian lady. She always tried to help me, prayed with me and everything. I still keep her phone number in my pocket. I just never have the courage to call her. I don't want her to know what I've become."

"I know what you mean."

"What do you like to do? Besides feed homeless people?"

I laughed. "Well, I like to play the violin."

"You do?" She put her hands inside her pockets. "Well, you'll have to play for me sometime."

"How about tomorrow?"

She smiled. "I'm looking forward to it."

When I slipped my key in the door I noticed something was different. Clothes were strewn across the floor. A black dress and…men's clothing. I heard sounds from behind Kelly's door and retreated to my room.

I knew this would be awkward.

I didn't have much time to contemplate it, because as soon as I got in my room and sat on my bed to scroll around on my phone, I fell asleep.

Thank God for my alarm clock or being on time for work would've been an impossibility. I rose up from my bed, still drained, and walked to the bathroom, opening the door. I jumped back seeing a tall man in just a towel, brushing his teeth.

"I'm so sorry!" I said closing the door.

He opened back the door, wrapping up his brushing and washing his mouth free from toothpaste. "It's all yours now," he said looking me up and down before walking past me back into Kelly's bedroom.

I walked in and locked the door behind me. I loved the feel of the warm shower and the clean scent of my shower gel. I put on a robe and left the shower, seeing Kelly and the man out in the kitchen.

"Hey Naomi," Kelly said waving me over. I hesitantly walked over. "This is my boyfriend Kyle Thomas. Kyle, this is my friend Naomi Beckford."

He wasn't really handsome, he was super tall, filled with tattoos, with a head that seemed too small for his body. But he was famous and rich and so I guess that was his appeal.

"Nice to meet you Kyle," I said extending my hand. "Thanks for letting me stay here."

"Nice to meet you too," he said taking it back and shaking it. He rubbed his thumb alongside my skin. I slowly pulled my hand from his. He averted his eyes from me and said to Kelly. "Anything for Kelly."

Kelly blushed and went to the kitchen and began cracking open and whipping some eggs. I retreated to my room and got dressed for work. I exited my room in my coat and hat.

"You're not going to eat breakfast?"

"Nah, I think I'll eat at work this morning," I said, pulling on my boots. "I'll see you guys later."

"Alright, bye," Kelly said.

Kyle waved at me, his gaze still intense. I went through the door. I brought my violin with me today, because I promised Ramona I'd play for her. I saw her sitting in her usual spot as I got close to the restaurant. I still had 30 minutes before work, and Sam had gotten into the routine of making sure something was prepared for her so that all I had to do was grab it and give it to her.

As I walked closer, I noticed she was already munching on a bagel. "Hey, you beat me to it, how'd you get food?"

"Your boss brought it out to me."

"He did?"

"Yes, nice man," she said, taking another bite.

I held up my violin case and smiled. "I brought it today." She gave me a warm smile before I asked, "Any song requests?"

"Do you know the one that they always play at weddings?"

I picked up my violin and played Canon in D. Ramona's face looked like that of a proud mother. *A mother.* I wondered what it truly meant to have one, to have someone who cried with you, laughed with you, who cared about your well-being more than theirs, who would tuck you in at nights, who would love you. I couldn't think about that now, it was useless. I stopped playing and she applauded as if I was at a school recital. I smiled, more out of embarrassment than happiness.

"You gonna be big one day. I know it." Ramona stood up. "Just you wait and see. You remind me of my friend's daughter, she used to play the piano."

"Thanks," I said putting my violin back in its case. "Well, I gotta head off to work now. I'll be back with dinner."

"See you later, Naomi."

"Always," I said back at her.

I walked over to the Riviera. No one was there, besides Sam.

"Morning, Sam. Thanks for bringing the food to Ramona this morning."

"No problem, kid." I realized that he would probably call me this for as long as I worked here. "Hey, I have something for you. I know it's long overdue." He handed me a name tag. It was gold tinted with NAOMI in capital letters. I stared at it for a moment.

"First job?"

"Yeah"

"What's a girl like you doing out on your own? You look like a NYU or Columbia student."

"A girl like me?"

"Yeah, well, you're smart, no doubt about that, and you look like you probably had some money."

I looked down, confirming his suspicions. "I can't go back home."

"Why not?" genuine curiosity filled his face.

I wouldn't tell him. "I just can't."

"Well, I'll take your word for it. I just don't want your parents to come barging in here one day looking for you. That would be bad business." The corners of his mouth rose into a big grin and he winked as he headed to the back to prepare the morning meals.

I smiled, just then Lisa entered. "Hey you're early."

"Yeah, I got a good jumpstart today."

"So, what did you do last night?"

"Umm, nothing." I wasn't going to tell her about Kelly and her superstar boyfriend. "I was tired, I fell asleep as soon as I got home."

"I'm having a party at my apartment on Friday. You wanna come?"

I wasn't really a party person, never had been. The other kids at my school rebelled against their parents by spending all of their money and throwing huge alcohol filled riots, while I stayed home to make scores that would become Academy Award winners.

But I couldn't turn down the first person to invite me somewhere; she would probably never speak to me again.

"Sure."

"Here's my address," she handed me a slip of paper.

"I'll be there." I would have never done anything like this before. No, I wouldn't have, because I was afraid of having fun around him, afraid that if I did, he would do something to change that. It was decided, I would go, I would have fun, and no one, nothing would take that opportunity from me, not this time.

"Kelly, guess what?" I said excitedly when I got home, I could see that Kyle was gone.

"What?" She had dark circles under her eyes. For the first time she didn't look pretty to me, as if the life had been sucked out of her.

"I got invited to a party!"

"Really?" She said somewhat disinterested, "That's good."

"What's wrong? Where's Kyle?"

"He's got an away game," She said dully, almost as if it was expected.

"You look...you guys didn't break up or anything, right?" I asked.

She chuckled and waved her hand and that's when I saw the blood in the crook of her arm. "No, of course not, he loves me."

"Your arm," I said coming to her side and grabbing it. She pulled away from me, but I reached for her arm again. "Let me see." I could see the different puncture wounds along her arm. Like someone taking... "You do drugs?" I asked incredulously.

"Relax, Naomi, what are you a DARE officer?"

I kept staring at the marks along her arm. "What is it? Heroin, Meth, Coke?"

She finally snatched her arm away from me. "Leave it alone, Naomi, I don't need you judging me. It's not like I do it ALL the time."

"Tell me!"

"It's heroin!" she yelled back at me.

"Why?" I said. "You have everything."

"You have one way of handling your pain and I have mine," she said before she went to her room, slamming the door.

Kelly slept in the next day, I only peeped in her door to make sure I could see her chest moving up and down. Then I left for work. I settled into my routine and brought Ramona breakfast.

"Good morning," I said.

"Morning," she said, unenthusiastically. She was laying down and didn't even attempt to move.

"What's wrong?" I asked.

"Just not feeling too good today."

"Will a song cheer you up?" I asked.

She gave a small smile. "Do you know the song, My Faith Looks Up to Thee?"

"No, I'm sorry I don't." I had never thought that Ramona was a religious person, I had never heard her speak about it.

"Well that's okay, I like anything you play," She said.

I gingerly picked up my violin wondering why on Earth my hands were shaking. Why were they so cold? My hands taking a more study grip to my bow started to play a song from Telemann, and Ramona slowly went to sleep without even touching her food.

The apartment wasn't hard to find. I stood in front of the door, nervous. *Stop being stupid! This is just a party*. My mind focused and I realized how cold it was, it seemed like spring was taking forever to kick in, even thought it was already mid-March. I knocked on the door, Lisa opened it flashing me her perfect smile.

"Hey you made it, come in."

I stepped in and looked around. There were about twenty people in this small cramped apartment. They all had large red plastic cups in their hand, cups filled with beer. Oh no! What had I been thinking?

"Hey, this is my friend from work, Naomi."

A muscular tanned brown man was in front of me. "Hi, Naomi."

"Hi." I said, my voice shaking.

Lisa walked away and curled up on a couch with a tall, lean black-haired man filled with tattoos. He turned back to look at me as the sound of Rihanna blared around us.

"My name's Cole, by the way."

My throat dried, I had no idea what to say.

"Let me guess, you're shy?"

I nodded my head slowly. *Relax Naomi! This is what happens at parties, you came here to have fun, remember that.*

"So, you want to dance? I know you didn't come in that dress to just drink punch."

I looked down at my cobalt blue dress. He was right I didn't come here to just drink punch.

"Sure, I'd like that," I said, my voice shaking.

He grabbed my hand then pulling me two steps over to where everyone was dancing. Slowly he put his hands on my waist. *This isn't hard, you know how to dance.* I let my body move to the music, as if in a trance. *Your first party and it only took eighteen years! I can't wait to tell Ramona how much fun this...*His hands were on my face now, his cold hands. I couldn't breathe now. *Relax Naomi! This is what happens at parties, you came here to have fun, remember that.* He was pulling my face towards his. *Relax! You came here to have fun, remember that.* But I wasn't remembering that as I bolted through the door.

My father died when I was five. Months after, mom was already out on the hunt. Every night she was gone, leaving me with any babysitter that was available. It was then that she enrolled me in my violin, piano, and various foreign language classes; she wanted me to have something to do after school and to become a classy sophisticated lady. Days were long, but I didn't complain, the classes were fun.

Tina was my sitter that day. Mom walked in the door that night, but she brought someone with her, a man.

"Hi, Tina, I'm home, you can leave now."

Tina was only too happy to cooperate, she collected her one hundred dollars, which no doubt was another deduction from my father's will and headed for the door.

"Well, now that we're alone, Naomi, sweetie, I have some very good news." She grabbed his hand and smiled, "We're getting married. Travis is gonna be your new daddy."

The dizziness began to wear off and my breathing slowed as I walked down the street. *Stupid!* I should have known that would happen. I got on the train, putting in headphones and trying to clear my head. When I got to our apartment, I pushed my key through the lock. The kitchen light was still on and I walked over to see Kyle sitting at the table scrolling through his phone.

"Hi," I said surprised. "Kelly said you had an away game."

"Yeah, I flew in not too long ago."

I nodded. "Welcome back."

He got out of his seat. "Kelly told me ya'll grew up together."

He towered over me, even in my heels. "Yeah. She's been a godsend for these past couple months. She's really been helping me get on my feet by staying here. I owe her."

He stepped closer. "What about me?"

I could feel my palms starting to sweat. "What about you?"

"You owe me too," he said shrugging. "It's my place."

"Yeah, I said thank you for letting me stay, I'm saving up to move out on my own in a few months."

"Nah, no pressure to leave or anything."

"Thanks," I said nervously, "Where's Kelly?" I asked.

"She's knocked out in her room. You know her."

"Is she alright?"

"Yeah, she's fine."

I turned to around to go to her room, before he grabbed me and smashed me to him, kissing my neck.

"Stop it!" I said trying to pull away from him, but he was strong, his grip firm on me. "Stop it!" I said scratching his face.

He cursed at me and pulled away. "Don't touch me!" I said. "I'll tell her! I swear I will!"

He laughed. "And even if you did, you think it makes a difference? I got plenty more where Kelly came from."

I backed away from him and went into my room locking the door. He didn't come after me, but I knew then that my stay here had to come to an end. I changed my clothes switched off all the lights, gazing out the window.

I had a beautiful view of Manhattan. But, it wasn't worth living in this close proximity to another monster. I settled down in bed, resting my head on the pillow, trying to calm my heart, wondering how I would tell Kelly and what Ramona was doing, had her day been boring or climatic like mine? Was she still not feeling well? She would probably want me to play something for her, she always did. Thunder rolled above me, and the clouds ruptured as water fell to the earth.

The next morning Kyle was gone. His stuff was still around, but at least he was out of the house, probably at practice. Kelly was on the couch.

"Hey, morning Naomi," she said, cheery. I'd gotten used to her two different moods.

"Hey." I went to the kitchen and turned on the kettle.

"How did the party go?"

"Not as great as planned. Not a party person, don't know why I thought I'd be."

"Aww you just need to be more social, you know what? You need a boyfriend, maybe I can set you up with one of Kyle's teammates."

His name made me recoil.

"What you don't want to date a ball player?" she said getting up from the couch.

"What do you know about Kyle?"

"What do you mean? I know tons of stuff about him," she said.

The kettle was getting ready to boil, I could hear it, but the whistle hadn't come.

"Kyle is a pig. He grabbed me, he kissed me last night. He said that I *owe* him because I live here."

I could see the different emotions registering in her eyes. Shock, hurt, then anger.

"You're lying."

"What?" I said staring back at her as the kettle started to whistle.

"You're lying. He wouldn't."

I could feel my face burning with anger and all I wanted to do was cry, but I didn't. I just turned around and turned off the stove.

"If you don't believe me then you're no better than everyone else who didn't believe you."

"Get out!" she screamed.

I nodded. "Don't say I didn't warn you."

I walked down the street with my suitcase and duffel bag. What was I gonna do now? Where am I gonna live? As I walked closer to the Riviera, I saw an ambulance.

Where's Ramona?

"Naomi!" Sam yelled from across the street. I looked both ways before running across to meet him.

"What's going on? Did someone at the restaurant get hurt?"

"No," he said, shaking his head. "It's Ramona. She didn't look too good this morning, and then she just started coughing and vomiting up blood, so I called the ambulance.

"Where is she?" I said frantically walking over to the back of the ambulance. She was on the stretcher being attended to. "Is she ok?" I asked a paramedic.

"Ma'am we're going to transport her to Gouverneur Health Center."

"Ok, but is she ok?"

"Ma'am, calm down, are you a family member?"

"No. But–"

"You can meet her at the hospital, she's unstable right now. We have to go."

I backed away from him feeling panic. I felt Sam's hand on my shoulder. "You can take the day to go see her."

"Thanks Sam," I said starting to walk back to the front of the restaurant where I'd left my luggage.

"What's with the suitcase?" he asked. "Leaving town?"

"No," I said. "My living arrangements are just...complicated."

"Complicated?"

I held my head. "Don't worry about it."

"I will when you're only 18."

"My roommate kicked me out. Her boyfriend got handsy with me and when I complained she kicked me out."

"Have you talked to your landlord? If you're paying rent then-"

"I wasn't paying rent. She was an old friend, letting me crash for free."

He rubbed his forehead. "I knew hiring you would get me in some type of trouble."

"Like I said it's not your problem, it's mine. I'll have to figure it out. I'll find a hotel or something."

"In the city?"

"I'll figure it out."

"Yeah and go broke in a week." He said. "Look, this is a total violation. But, I can let you stay here in the restaurant for one week, that's it. After that, you gotta figure it out."

I nodded. "Thanks, Sam."

"One week."

"One week."

I was at the hospital in forty minutes; I had to wait for the train this time.

"Hi, do you know what room Ramona's in?" I said frantically

"I'm sorry, what do you need?" The receptionist said.

"I need to know what room Ramona's in!" She was a little too calm.

"Can I have a last name please?"

Last name? I didn't know Ramona's last name! "I'm sorry I don't know her last name, Ramona's not common; can you just look it up?" I was starting to lose my patience. She eyed me and started to type on her computer.

"Ramona Turner. Room 321."

"Thanks," I said racing for the elevator. After receiving guidance every step of the way from the nurses, I stood before Ramona's room. Taking a deep breath, I knocked. No answer. I knocked again. Still nothing. Opening the door, I peered in, Ramona was there, but she wasn't the Ramona I remembered, this Ramona's skin was black as tar, tubes ran from her body, her lips were chapped, her hair a mess, she looked weak, helpless, not like my Ramona at all. She looked over at me.

"Hey," she said lightly, almost like a whisper. I couldn't speak.

"Well, ain't you gonna sit?"

I made my way slowly to a chair beside her. "What's wrong with you, Ramona?" She took a deep breath and closed her eyes.

"You know life is all about choices, child. I used to live in Alabama and I played piano for my church; I even used to sing on the choir. Well when I was just about your age I met this boy, Henry Jackson. I was determined to be his main thing, and I was. I would do anything for him. So, when he told me to run away with him to Chicago, I didn't hesitate, not even for one minute," She laughed, her voice cracking.

"When we was in Chicago, in our small ol' apartment, Henry was always gone and money was disappearing. He was hooked on heroin. He asked me to take it too, at first, I said no, but after a while I gave in, I thought I was doing it to make him happy; soon it was making me happy too. I lost everything, Henry died of a drug overdose and I moved here homeless. I got real sick one day and I went to a clinic and I'll never forget that nurse, Michelle, she looked at me real sad and said, 'you have AIDS,' I cried for about three days," Ramona put my hands in hers now, "You see, child, life is all about choices."

I fiddled nervously with a bottle on the dresser. "Ramona, how come you've never asked me why I'm on my own?"

"I figured if you was going to tell me, then I would wait for that. You never asked me."

She was right, I didn't. I wanted to tell her, but the words wouldn't come out.

"I didn't have a choice," I whispered. She looked at me now, her brown eyes piercing me.

"I know someone. I have her number here," she said reaching for it on her dresser. "It's one of the only things I've kept all these years."

"Who's Lorna?" I asked.

"The lady I told you I used to work with. She's a nice Christian lady, she'll take good care of you, I promise."

I shook my head confused. "Why didn't you call her all these years?"

"First it was because I couldn't get clean, then it was just the shame of her seeing me this way." She sighed. "But, you need her. Please call her when you can. Promise me."

"Ramona, I can't-"

"Promise me."

"Ok, I promise, I'll give her a call."

She laid back now, exhausted, "I'm so sorry for everything that happened to you Naomi. Really I am."

I slept there that night. Ramona coughed and wheezed throughout the night. At 2 am I woke up to her laughter, silver streaks streaming down her face.

"I thought you wouldn't want me anymore. Oh, Lord, I thought you didn't want me anymore."

"Ramona, who are you talking to?"

She looked at me as if I was stupid, or blind. "He said he forgives me, he wants me."

"Who wants you?"

"Sweet Jesus."

Right then she began to sing, I didn't know the song, something about "every hour I need thee". She turned to me, "You can go with me too."

"Go where?"

"Heaven! Child, where else?"

"No, Ramona, you're staying here." I pleaded with her.

"I don't want to stay here. I wanna go now, but I want you to know you can come with me."

"I can't go to heaven with you Ramona," I said curtly.

"Sure, you can, child," she looked straight into my eyes "You know he loves you, even though I know you been through, he loves you."

Then she began to sing, "My faith looks up to thee, thou Lamb of Calvary, Savior divine! Now hear me while I pray, take all my guilt away; O let me from this day be wholly thine." She sang and sang, her face beaming in a smile.

"Bye, Naomi, I'll see you later."

"No, Ramona."

"Bye, Naomi, I'll see you later." She held my hand and she went, her face still smiling. I sat frozen as the nurses whirled in the room and the knots in my soul nearly squeezed the life out of me.

2 DELIVERANCE

"Have you filled out an application for Harvard yet?" I looked at my mother, her jewels gleaming.

"Mom, I already told you I don't want to go to Harvard." I shouldn't be this hard on her; she just wanted me to go to a good school, one that would impress her friends, and one that would catapult me to the forefront of high society.

"What about Princeton? Travis will pay for anywhere you choose."

"I don't need his money," I said harshly.

My mother moved now to sit on the side of my bed. "You know it wouldn't hurt for you to be nice to Travis after all he's done for us."

I stayed silent, it was for the best. I couldn't tell her, it would kill her, to know she had married a monster. It had stopped six years now, he knew that if he had continued his transgressions would have been evident for all to see. Plus, it was clear that he liked them young. I was grateful, if only for that.

"So, Melissa tells me that Tyler asked you out…and you said no. Why Naomi? He would be good for you."

Melissa was one of my mother's fellow housewives. Her son Tyler, however, had been a thorn in my side, always trying to buy my affection.

"No, I don't think so."

"Well Naomi! You never go out with anyone! You don't go on the weekends with friends, and it's starting to look bad!" She was angry now.

I glared at her, trying to control my own irritation as well. "I'm sorry." I said flatly.

This only drove her over the edge. "It's in the past, Naomi! You need to get over it! I've gotten over it!"

My eyes narrowed, Goosebumps forming on my skin. "Gotten over what?"

Her eyes became wide and she didn't speak as I came to stand directly in front of her.

"You knew, didn't you," I whispered.

Her silence confirmed my accusation. I always heard people say that I had lost my father at a tender age, and in that moment, I realized that I had also lost my mother.

April 14th. I hadn't spoken to Kelly again and neither had she called me. I was angry with her, but I also felt scared for her, scared she would overdose someday, scared that she was with Kyle. I checked to see how she was doing on Instagram, but it seems to all be the same. More selfies, more courtside pictures. The only difference is that it was a different court now. I guess she had moved on from Kyle to another player.

Days at the Riviera were long; I had made them that way. I went to help Sam early in the morning and stayed long after my ten o' clock to six o' clock shifts were over. Sam eventually convinced me to play my violin for the customers. Good business, he said.

I walked into the Riviera, "Hey Sam, good morning."

"Morning, kid," he said sliding a card across the table, "Happy Birthday."

"You remembered," I said smiling.

"Yep, the computer always reminds me," This was the humor that Sam and I shared. "So how old are you now?"

"Nineteen."

"Ahh, I remember when I was nineteen; it was just about 3 years ago."

"Yeah, how about 30 years ago?"

"Ha, ha, get back to work before I fire you," He grinned wide before heading back to the kitchen.

That day went by in slow motion. More obnoxious customers, most of them not even taking the time to say thank you; at least they left good tips. My savings were quickly dwindling, now that I was saying nights at hotels. My budget consisted of hotel fees, food, and metro tickets; I wouldn't even buy myself a new cell phone. I only had my iPhone without a SIM card and a trac phone I used for emergencies. Each day, after six I was grateful to be able to pick up my violin and sit at the center of the restaurant and just simply play. I would get many requests through the night ranging from Bach to Barber's Adagio for Strings to Dirty Orchestra by Black Violin, that last one being requested by none other than the NYU students. I left work late as usual, the air had gotten warmer and the ice no longer whipped around my face. Every day, walking to the Riveria was a numbing experience because Ramona wasn't there.

My throat hurt this morning, as I readied myself for work. I headed to work today, once again fighting the urge not to look in the spot where Ramona used to be. I came early every day for work, just to stay busy. Lisa arrived, and we worked tirelessly throughout the day.

"Guess what, Jay got a gig at Table 50." Jay was Lisa's boyfriend and her route to fame and fortune. I felt bad for her, she didn't realize that sometimes all the riches in the world couldn't buy her happiness.

"That's great."

"Yeah, well he's really excited and..." the door opened, Lisa was looking at the man coming in. "Wow, look at that."

I couldn't blame her, he was gorgeous. He was six feet tall, chocolate brown skin and deep dimples. He sat down, reading something, I was staring.

"Go take his order!" Lisa whispered.

"No, why don't you?" I whispered back.

"I have a boyfriend and you're in desperate need of one since you and Cole didn't work out."

I glared at her, I hated when she brought that night up. I was positive that she would have dropped it when I lied and told her that I was feeling nauseous that day.

"You are going to take his order, Naomi,"

She smiled at me then and ran to another customer. I was trapped. I took a deep breath and walked over to him.

"Hi, my name is Naomi, can I take your order?"

His brown eyes locked with mine then, I swallowed, feeling my throat burn.

"Yes, um do you have any recommendations?" His voice was hypnotizing.

"Umm, sure, well the crepes are really good."

"Alright, crepe it is."

"What filling?"

"I guess chicken."

"Okay, coming right up." Suddenly I caught a glimpse of what he was reading, a bible. The attraction was now lost. I put his order in the computer and waited for Sam to call me. The crowd wasn't heavy at this time, so his order was ready in ten minutes. I headed back to the table.

"Here you go," I said putting his plate on the table, "Enjoy your lunch."

Turning to leave, I heard his velvet voice, "Um....sorry miss, I just have a question? Would the owner mind if I stayed for a while, and studied?"

"Study?" I glanced at his bible.

"Yeah, I'm a seminary student."

"Oh, I'm sure that would be fine."

"Can I ask you another question?"

"Sure." Why was he asking so many questions?

"Do you attend a church?"

What! What kind of question was that? "No, I don't."

"Why not?" genuine curiosity flowed from his coffee colored eyes.

"I don't believe in God."

"Would you mind if I asked why?

I felt angry even though his face was calm. "Yes, I would mind," I said sharply.

"Well, you're a little feisty for someone who's so pint-sized," he said exposing gleaming white teeth and his deep dimples. Despite being momentarily stunned by this, I was livid, this guy was unbelievable.

"Pint-sized." I said, my jaw tightening.

My obvious anger seemed to entertain him, his body shook with laughter. "Look, I'm sorry I just wanted to ask some questions."

"Well, I'm not in the mood for questions. However, you can continue your studying," I said walking away.

I made Lisa cover his table until he left, flashing me a dimpled smile and leaving me a twenty-dollar tip.

By Sunday morning I had developed a cough. It hurt to take a breath. I sprayed my throat with chloraseptic and took as much cough drops as I possibly could, so that Sam wouldn't send me home. I switched places with Lisa today and took the welcome desk today, thank God, the less interaction with customers food, the better.

But eventually it got so bad that Sam wanted me to stay away from touching the menus.

"Jeez, Naomi, that cough is getting bad. You should go see a doctor," Sam looked at me as I struggled for air.

"No, I'll be fine," I said in between a few coughs.

"Why don't you just play your violin for the rest of the day?"

"Okay," I said weakly.

I took my violin out of the case and tightened my bow and began to play. I played the song I had heard in my dreams last night, dreams of myself in a cage, surrounded by darkness, a man with eyes like a blazing fire approached me.

"Naomi, come with me." He said softly

"No."

"I can let you out."

"I can do it myself."

He looked at me with pity. "Let me help you, Naomi. Only I can do it."

I opened my eyes; Nathaniel Bennett was standing in front of me.

"That was beautiful. Who's the composer?""

"What are you doing here?" I said coldly.

"Well isn't it obvious? I came here to eat."

"Well, have a seat; someone will be with you shortly." I retorted.

"Not until you answer two questions for me," He smiled wide now, his dimples making indentations on his skin.

"What is with you and these questions?" I fumed.

"What's your name?" He said ignoring me.

"Naomi Beckford."

"Who's the composer?"

"Me. Happy? Go take a seat."

He turned and sat at a table that faced my direction. Was it possible that someone could infuriate you so much? I resumed playing now, suddenly nervous now that he was there. He ate quietly, reading his bible. He rose from his seat watching me with a smile on his face.

"Bye, pint."

I glared at him, not saying anything. He bent down and put something in my violin case and left. Curiosity got the best of me and I went to my violin case, there was a tiny green book. The Gospel of John.

It had been two weeks and he hadn't come back. Not that I was waiting for him. My cold got worse, it became the flu. Sam had indefinitely sent me on sick leave. I spent my days in my hotel room coughing and sweating on my bed. I'd found out yesterday that Kelly had died. Found out on social media. Overdose. I cried the whole night.

I was almost out of money. I only had enough to last me one more night in this hotel. I couldn't ask Sam for another week to stay at the restaurant, so I could save up. I had to do something, or I would end up homeless. I reached into my wallet and pulled out the piece of paper Ramona had given me.

Lorna.

I rested my head against the backboard of the bed. I am really going to call a perfect stranger and ask to stay with her? Yes.

Yes, I am.

I have no choice.

I dialed the number and listened to the phone ring. Please, let it go to voicemail. Please.

"Hello," I heard a soft voice say on the other end.

"Hi," I cleared my throat. "Hi is this Lorna?"

"Yes, this is Lorna."

"Hi, Lorna, my name is Naomi Beckford, I'm a friend of Ramona, she gave me your number."

"Ramona, oh gosh I haven't seen her in years! How is she?"

I took a deep breath. "Actually, she um...she passed away about a month ago."

There was silence on the other end, before she came back on with a shaky voice. "What happened to her?"

I told her about Ramona's drug addiction and homelessness, about how we'd met and that she'd died from complications from AIDS. "She felt ashamed to tell you, but she mentioned your name before she passed, she sang to God and before I knew it she was gone. She was smiling."

I could hear Lorna sniffling. "Thank you for telling me."

"You're welcome. Ramona asked me to call you because she wants you to help me." I cleared my throat. "I didn't want to have to make this call...it's hard for me...but, I'm 19 and I'm on my own and I don't have to stay. I've been trying to survive off of waitressing and tips, but umm.... It's not enough and I'm afraid I'll be out on the streets."

"No, you're not," she said resolutely. "Get on a train and come to the Jay Street station, I'll pick you up from there."

The car ride to Lorna's house was quiet. I was tempted to fall asleep, but I was too anxious. Her house was a two-story white house. It looked like the homes you saw on TV. I rolled my suitcase in, quick to get out of the cold. Lorna closed the door and looked at me.

"Well here we are. Well, you can stay in the guest room upstairs, you'll have your own bathroom and everything."

"Thank you."

"Are you a user?"

Well she didn't waste any time. "No, I'm not, I don't even drink."

"Good. Well, some rules apply to living here."

"That's understandable."

"Yes, well, you'll get a key after some time, but I'd like for you not to stay out past twelve."

"Ok."

"No people over unless you speak to me first."

"Yes, ma'am."

"And we'll go to church every week."

My eyes went wide.

"It won't kill you," she responded.

I didn't say anything. Yes, it would.

"So, tell me about yourself Naomi."

"Umm…. there's not much to tell. I'm not that interesting."

"That's what everyone says, have a seat, and just tell me anything."

I followed her to take a seat in the kitchen.

"Are you hungry?"

"No ma'am."

"Ok, well, tell me something."

What do I tell her? "My name is Naomi Beckford. I've lived in Long Island most of my life."

"Yes..." she waited for me to add something, "You came in with a violin case, I'm guessing you're a dedicated musician."

"I guess."

"You guess? Let me hear something."

"I have to get my violin out of my suitcase."

"Do you play piano? We have one in the living room."

She led me to a black grand piano. "My husband and my daughter were musicians." I remember Ramona telling me that Lorna's daughter played the piano.

"Were musicians?"

"Yes, drunk driver hit them about five years ago." Her voice showed no signs of bitterness. "Okay, so entertain me." She said switching to a happier tone.

I sat at the piano; taking a deep breath I let my hand run gently over the keys, as if putting the key back in my memory. It had been so long since I'd played. I started to play Brahms Piano Sonata No. 1 in C Major. When I finished she just smiled at me. *See there is something interesting about you.* Why was I always able to know what she was thinking or about to say? It was as if I had known her all my life.

"Now I'm excited to hear you play that violin. Go get it out for me."

I went back to suitcase and pulled out my violin. I played the Theme Song from Schindler's List; I've always loved John Williams. She clapped delightfully as I finished.

"I know what you're thinking, why is this woman letting me inside her house? Is it because she's a lonely widow? Am I right?"

Actually, she had hit it right on the head. "Yes."

"Naomi, I used to be just like you, a drifter, not because I was a drug addict or an alcoholic. My mother was a junkie and she couldn't take care of me. I went from foster home to foster home and when I turned eighteen, I saw my opportunity for freedom. I would still be out there if it hadn't been for someone who pulled me out." There was still no bitterness. Strange.

"But why me?"

"That's a question I'll never be able to fully answer," she sighed, "God laid it on my heart."

She looked at me and laughed. "Now you really think I'm crazy." Again, she was right.

"I guess I'm glad he did," I said sarcastically.

Living with Lorna was okay, more than okay, my flu was almost eradicated within two days, she constantly fed me and for the two days I had been here we stayed up until one in the morning talking. We spent hours finishing each other's thoughts and sentences; everything was kind of…well…perfect. Just like home, except for incessant talk about Jesus and God and the Holy Spirit. But I dealt with it; she said her son was coming over on Saturday. That should at least put a momentary break on Jesus talk.

"Mrs. Lorna, I can help you with dinner."

"You want to help, that's very nice."

"So, what do you need?"

"You make anything you want."

We spent the next two hours laughing, stirring, joking, and frying. A door opened as I was adding some touches to the cake I had made.

"Mama, I'm home." I voice echoed from the front of the house.

I turned my head to Nathaniel Bennett entering the kitchen.

"What are you doing here?" We both said simultaneously. However, my voice sounded more edgy than his.

"This happens to be my house."

"No," Lorna said, pinching Nathaniel's arm, "This is my house."

I continued to stare him down.

"So, Pint was your visitor? Why didn't you tell me?"

I rolled my eyes. "Because it's none of your business who I let in my house, that's why." *Tell him, Lorna.*

"I'm going to go upstairs to freshen up." Lorna walked away leaving Nathaniel and I to face each other.

"This would be my luck for you to be Lorna's son."

"I don't believe in luck."

"Did you and Ramona set this up?"

"Who's Ramona?"

He really didn't know her. This is crazy.

"I didn't know you two knew each other," Lorna said as she walked back down the stairs. Nathaniel and I turned to her. She walked into the kitchen and grabbed the bowl of salad and put it on the dining table, "So how did you two meet?" She said getting the rest of the food.

"He shows up at my job and harasses me." He shot me a look, I gladly returned one.

"Don't worry mom, I harass everyone there."

Lorna now finished setting the table. "Come on you two, come and eat." The dinner was good, as always. The only problem was that Nathaniel sat right across from me grinning as he saw my obvious discomfort. He was obnoxious, irritating and a perfect gentleman. He helped us clean up with no complaints; he even hugged and kissed his mom when he left. He was not what I expected. Not what I expected at all.

I had to go to church today. Learning to wake up on Sundays was going to be hard. Learning to sit through an entire service was going to be harder. I learned that Nathaniel's father had been the founder of the church; however, another man Rev. Jones was now the pastor. The church was nice and lively, most of the people smiled as I walked in and asked Lorna who I was. Most of the girls watched Nathaniel. Nathaniel spoke again today on deliverance.

"So how did you think service was?" Nathaniel asked me after church.

"Do you really want me to answer that?"

He laughed, "No I guess not."

"You have a way with words, you should really think about becoming a politician or something."

He chuckled. "No, politics isn't really my thing."

"Oh, the girls will be disappointed; it looks like most of them were looking forward to becoming the first lady."

"First of all, I'm only twenty-one, not quite ready for marriage yet, I want to finish school, meet the right woman."

"Shouldn't be too hard, you have a lot to pick from."

He smirked, "Your favorite instrument is the violin, right?"

"Yes…" I said confused.

"So, if they told you that you had to play one instrument for the rest of your life, you'd pick the violin any day?"

"Yeah, but if there was no violin, I'd pick anything rather than not be able to play at all."

"But, you'd still be dreaming of the violin."

"Morning Sam."

"Hey, kid, you're back and better."

"Yup, so can I have my job back?"

"It never went anywhere," He smiled, "But get working before I have to fire you."

I fell right back into the rhythm of waiting tables, it felt like it had been months, it was more like four days. Lisa had a lot to catch up on, Jay got another gig, she was going to a party on Friday, and she decided to go design school. She showed me a few sketches, she was actually really good.

"Yeah, I kinda gave up on it, my parents always said, 'Do something better with your life, be a doctor or a lawyer', and I just couldn't be that for them."

"I'm happy for you."

"So, when are you gonna do something about that music?"

I laughed, "Do what?"

"I don't know, join a symphony or something. I've heard the New York Philharmonic a few times."

Being a part of the New York Philharmonic had been my dream since I was little; playing with people like Leonard Bernstein to helping make Academy Award winning scores.

"I couldn't," I busied myself with organizing menus to avoid her face.

"Why not?"

"They have college graduates auditioning for them every day, why would they choose me?"

"Because you're amazing! That's why."

I rolled my eyes.

"I can't even believe I'm debating this with you," she said incredulously. She looked out the window. "Look who came to make your day better." Nathaniel was walking around the corner.

"Oh no... Lisa...tell him," my mind was flustered as I was walking to the kitchen, "Tell him I'm not here."

"Oh no, I'm not," she said laughing.

"Please don't do this to me," I said hiding my face as he entered.

I could hear his voice. "Hi, yes I would like lemonade and a crepe with fruit filling." *Another crepe, come on be a little diverse.*

Lisa entered after a long silence. "I believe that you'll go serve him."

"Why are being like this? He's so annoying."

"Naomi, stop being stupid. You'll thank me for this later."

"Crepe is ready!" Sam called out.

"Go," Lisa ordered.

Food leveled on my right arm, I walked out. I set it down next to him, he was reading his bible. Good, maybe he won't notice me.

"Naomi, I was wondering where you were." Dang.

"Enjoy your lunch," I said walking away.

"No, wait, aren't you going to make friendly conversation with me?"

"No, I'm kind of working now; I have other customers to attend to."

He made a show of looking around the restaurant. There was no one there. "Not many people come to restaurants at ten in the morning."

I narrowed my eyes, "What are you doing here, anyway?"

"Just came to harass you, pint," he said nonchalantly.

I looked around before I sat in the seat directly in front of him. "No more pint."

"What do you mean no more pint?"

"We have to make a deal for you to stop calling me that stupid name!"

"I like it," He said innocently.

"Well, I don't," I snapped.

"Okay, I'll stop calling you pint under one condition."

"What condition?" I said suspiciously.

"Guessing that you didn't throw away my present, we can read the book of John together."

"Together? As in me and you? I don't think so. By the way, how can you be so sure that I didn't throw away your present?"

"I don't know, but I'm hoping you didn't. And no, I'm being adamant; we have to read it together."

"Why? Do you think I'm incapable of understanding the Bible?"

"No, that's not it. But if you'd rather me give you a quiz on John, I mean I'll be happy to suffice. But I'm warning you, my test might be extremely difficult."

I sucked in a breath. This was going to be horrible. "Fine, but if I have to suffer through reading the bible with you, then you have to do one more thing."

"And what's that?"

"You have to stop coming to the Riviera."

He laughed now, "This is a public place!"

"I'm quite aware of that. I guess I could allow you to come when I'm off hours."

He looked at me for a long time now, debating whether to accept my offer. He sighed loudly, "Fine. We'll do a chapter a day, every day."

He grabbed the takeout box I had purposely put next to him and scooped his crepe inside.

"How many chapters are there?"

He smiled now, his eyes gleaming, "Twenty-one."

"In the beginning was the Word, and the Word was with God, and the Word was God. The same was in the beginning with God. All things were made by him; and without him was not any thing made that was made. In him was life; and the life was the light of men. And the light shineth in darkness; and the darkness comprehended it not."

"What does that mean? Who was the Word?" I asked.

"Jesus is the Word."

Nathaniel kept his word; we started reading John the very next day. So here I was around the kitchen counter reading what Nathaniel referred to as "the Word of God".

"So, if he was God, how could he be with God?"

"There's the Trinity. Father, Son, Holy Ghost."

"Jesus is the Son." At least I knew that much.

"Yeah, well they are three distinct figures, but one God."

"One God, with three people, that makes a lot of sense," I said sarcastically.

"Hold up your hand."

"What?"

"Just do it."

I held up my hand slowly. He looked at it for a moment before he spoke. "Your hand has five fingers, right."

"Yes."

"Well, all those five fingers are independent of your hand; however, it still remains one hand. What would your fingers do if they were on their own?"

Good explanation. He was better than I thought. He continued to read, his voice flowing with every syllable.

"…Behold the Lamb of God, which taketh away the sin of the world…"

You shouldn't be so mean to him, even if he's subjecting you to a mild form of torture.

"...Phillip, like Andrew and Peter, was from the town of Bethsaida. Phillip found Nathanael---"

"Your name is in here," I grinned wide, "This wouldn't happen to be the reason you wanted to read this book."

He chuckled. "No, but it's a definite plus. Your name is in another book in the bible, we could read it later."

"No, I think I'll pass on that."

We continued to read in silence with Lorna shifting in and out watching every so often.

"So, did you like it?"

"Great literary piece, nothing too interesting." I looked at him for a reaction, I was being mean again.

He didn't show any anger. Instead the corners of his mouth turned upward. "You're an atheist, am I correct?"

"Yes, I am," I said leaning back on the chair.

"Are you sure?"

What does he mean am I sure?

"Yes, I'm quite sure."

"I beg to differ, I think that you believe he exists, you just choose not to believe in him for whatever your reason may be."

I glared at him now. He lost the opportunity for me to be nice to him.

"You wanna know something about your God?" I said my voice quivering with anger, "He's a sick person who enjoys the torture of the less fortunate. He doesn't care about you or me!"

"Really, he doesn't?" Nathaniel said challenging me.

"No, he doesn't, or he wouldn't have killed off your father and your sister!"

His face grew hard. I had gone too far, I should apologize but I couldn't, not when I was so angry.

"You're wrong," He said his voice low with emotion, "He kept me alive."

He started to walk to the door. I obviously hit a soft spot.

"Wait!" I called out.

He turned to face me. "You're not angry at him? Not even a little bit?"

He looked at me, his eyes boring into mine.

"I used to be." And with that, he left.

Nathaniel surprisingly came back the next day. He said he wasn't going to pass up this opportunity to teach me the Bible. "I'm not going to be able to call you Pint or go to the Riviera; there's no way you're getting out of this," he said yesterday. So here I was today, suffering through John 3. It wasn't that this wasn't interesting; it was just very difficult to understand. How could a man be born again? What constituted a spiritual birth? Surely saying a simple prayer couldn't do that.

"...I tell you the truth; no one can enter the kingdom of God unless he is born of water and the Spirit..."

This wasn't making any sense.

"Wait!" I said impatiently, "I don't understand. How is someone born of the Spirit?"

Nathaniel smiled patiently. "Hold on, it's going to be explained a little further."

Why couldn't Jesus just speak plainly; instead of lacing his words with mysteries?

"...Just as Moses lifted up the snake in the desert, so the son must be lifted up, that everyone who believes in him may have eternal life. For God so loved the world that he gave his one and only Son, that whoever believes in him shall not perish but have eternal life. For God did not send his Son into the world to condemn the world, but to save the world through him. Whoever believes in him is not condemned, but whoever believes in him not is condemned already because he has not believed in the name of God's one and only son.'"

"So, I'm condemned if I don't accept him," I said coolly. He just looked at me. Evidently, I had answered my own question.

"So, the murderers, thieves, perverts, and that stupid drunk driver can go to heaven if they believe in this," I held up the Bible angrily. "But I don't go, because I can't love a God who's indifferent towards me."

"He's definitely not indifferent."

"Yeah, I'm quite sure." I said sarcastically.

"You're forgetting that your sin is no greater than theirs. Every lie, every moment of lust or envy, holds the same weight to God. We're no better than a murder, a pervert, or that drunk driver."

He was calm, I wasn't.

"You can't compare me to those people."

"Well if you're so high and mighty; then save yourself." He was challenging me.

"Save myself from what?"

"Stop messing up, stop sinning," He threw his hands up. "If you're so strong, then do it yourself."

"Humans are fallible." I said sharply.

"Exactly, you need someone who's pure to pay the atonement for your mistakes. He would have still died if you were the only person on earth who had messed up, he loves you that much. All he asks is a simple thing, for you to believe and to follow him."

It seemed like a simple task, nothing too hard. I stared at Nathaniel unsure of what to say, I wasn't a perfect person, I had never professed to be. But I wasn't like the others, the criminals, the heartless, like my family.

"I can't." I said leaving the table.

"Hi, I'm Naomi, are you ready to order?" I asked a customer.

"No, not quite, I'll just have a glass of water for now." They said flashing their hand at me.

At the sound of that word, fragments of last night's bible study ran through my mind. "...Where can you get this living water? ... Jesus answered and said 'Everyone who drinks this water will be thirsty again, but whoever drinks the water that I give him will never thirst. The water I give him will become in him a spring of water welling up to eternal life."

Ramona wanted me to meet her in eternity, but I couldn't, I couldn't be with her if that meant I had to accept the person that took her away. Was Jesus the only one who could take away the hurt that I had buried deep inside? Was he even strong enough?

"So, how are you enjoying bible study?" Lorna asked with a smile pulling at her lips.

"I enjoy church more." I said jokingly.

She laughed and looked at the piano. "My daughter Michelle and I used to play this game." She said reminiscing.

"What type of game?"

"She used to play songs she wrote, and I would guess what they were about."

"Cool!" I went to the piano. "Okay, what should I play."

"Just play anything; play something you're feeling, or a memory."

I brushed my hands over the keys. I began to play, thoughts flooding my memory. The first night in the shelter, the day after the party, dark skin, tubes, a faint beeping sound. I hadn't realized I had stopped playing until Lorna interrupted.

"It's about Ramona."

I just stared at her. I always knew she had been able to be on the same wavelength as me, but this was just too good.

"She meant something to you." She said. Her voice held no uncertainty.

She was my first real friend when I moved to the city." I whispered.

"Did you cry?" She asked.

"What?" My voice was a little stronger.

"Did you cry? It always helps when you cry a little."

I had never thought about this, why hadn't I? Why would Lorna even ask me this?

"No, I didn't," was all I could say.

I never had.

"Teacher, this woman was caught in the act of adultery. In the law Moses commanded us to stone such women? Now what do you say? They were using this question as a trap, in order to have a basis for accusing him. But Jesus bent down and started to write on the ground with his finger. When they kept on questioning him, he straightened up and said to them, 'If any one of you is without sin, let him be the first to throw a stone at her.' Again, he stooped down and wrote on the ground. At this, those who heard began to go away one at a time, the older ones first, until only Jesus was left, with the woman still standing there. Jesus straightened up and asked her, 'Woman, where are they? Has no one condemned you?' 'No one, sir,' she said. 'Then neither do I condemn you,' Jesus declared. 'Go now and leave your life of sin.'"

"Nathaniel," I said slowly, considering my words. "If you had the chance, would you kill the drunk driver?"

He looked up at me. "No, I wouldn't."

He meant it, I could tell.

"Would you think I'm a horrible person if I would want to kill the person that did that to me?"

"No, it's a natural feeling. At first I was so mad when they died." He looked down possibly remembering what had happened.

"What happened that day?"

"My sister had an audition at Julliard," He smiled a little. "She was so excited. My father and I went with her while my mom stayed behind to throw this huge congrats party." He sucked in a breath, unsure of how to go on. "We were on our way and the light turned green and all I remember is the car slamming in to us and the car flipped over a couple times. I hit my head and woke up in a hospital room."

"I'm sorry."

"No, don't be," He looked off a little, like he wasn't talking to me. "Sometimes I wish I had gone with them, sometimes I get a little jealous that they got to see him before I did."

"Why would God let that happen to someone like you?" I said absentmindedly.

"Like me?"

"You're perfect, everyone loves you, you do everything right."

Nathaniel erupted in laughter. "Believe me I'm nowhere near perfect. Ask my mom she'll tell you that I was a pretty rough person to handle, especially when I was a teenager. And not everyone likes me," he said as he stared back at me.

I was suddenly uneasy; I got up from around the table. "It's not that I don't like you, you're just so annoying sometimes."

His lips turned up into a smile. "Annoying, how so?"

"Well for one, you always called me pint."

"*Called* you pint, I believe that's past tense."

He was right, I had nothing. Truth was I couldn't like him because he always caused me to question the things I had held on to. I didn't want to crumble, I didn't want to be shaken, I wouldn't be melted by the words of Jesus.

But against my better judgment I held out my hand and he gripped it in a shake. Truce.

"Sam, can I ask you a question?" I had gone to work earlier today, Sam was preparing some croissants.

"Yeah, sure."

"Even if it's personal?" I said a little nervously.

"Depends on how personal," He said finally giving me all of his attention.

"Do...you...believe in God?"

He quizzically at me, "Yeah, sure, I do. I mean I was sort of raised Catholic."

"Sort of?"

"Well, my mother never really went to church, but when we went to France every summer she would read me stories from the bible. Why do you ask?"

"No reason."

"Do you believe in him?"

I looked at his honey eyes and I couldn't lie to him. "Je ne sais pas," I whispered. *I don't know.*

We had finished John 15 and Nathaniel was getting something to eat while I turned the TV to a Spanish channel.

"You speak Spanish?" He called from behind me.

"Yeah."

"And French, I heard you speak to the chef a couple times. And I'm guessing that's not the only language you can speak, is it?"

"German." I said as a matter of fact. "The others I can't speak fluently."

"And what are the others?"

"Portuguese and Chinese."

"Wow," I could tell he was impressed. "I've always wanted to learn a foreign language."

"Really, why didn't you?"

"Never had the focus, when I was in high school I was just focused on other things. How did you learn all those languages?"

"My mom made me take classes."

"You never talk about her, how is she?"

I didn't say anything.

"That bad?"

"That bad."

"What about your dad?"

"He died when I was five." I knew my voice sounded emotionless. I had, had enough questioning about my family. Time to change the subject.

"I could teach you, if you want."

"All right."

"So which language do you want to learn?"

"I guess French."

"Why French?"

"First I'm trying to go on a missions trip with my school to Haiti and I was hoping that you'd let me come back to the Riviera."

I laughed, "Not until we finish John."

"Yes! Finally, a change of heart." I just stared at him because those words were becoming true.

Lorna and I played our game just about every night. She always guessed my songs; the ones about work, about living here, about bible study, or church. I had now raised enough to get my own apartment, but I wasn't ready to leave yet. I bought a cell phone instead with some of the money I had saved. Sam was happy about that. I walked to Lorna's house today, humming a tune, one that I was planning to probably quiz Lorna on tonight after bible study. Nathaniel arrived at the house at 7:30 after school. We quickly moved to the table to read after he had eaten dinner.

"Okay so today is John 19. Tell me what happened in the last chapter.

"They arrested Jesus and questioned him, and the people chose Barnabas over Jesus." I said like it was no big deal.

"Alright so here we go."

Then Pilate took Jesus and had him flogged. The soldiers twisted together a crown of thorns and put it on his head. They clothed him in a purple robe and went up to him again and again, saying, "Hail, king of the Jews!" And they struck him in the face. Once more Pilate came out and said to the Jews, "Look, I am bringing him out to you to let you know that I find no basis for a charge against him." When Jesus came out wearing the crown of thorns and the purple robe, Pilate said to them, "Here is the man!" As soon as the chief priests and their officials saw him, they shouted, "Crucify! Crucify!" But Pilate answered, "You take him and crucify him. As for me, I find no basis for a charge against him."

How could they find a charge against him? He was innocent.

The Jews insisted, "We have a law, and according to that law he must die, because he claimed to be the Son of God." When Pilate heard this, he was even more afraid, and he went back inside the palace. "Where do you come from?" he asked Jesus, but Jesus gave him no answer. "Do you refuse to speak to me?" Pilate said. "Don't you realize I have power either to free you or to crucify you?" Jesus answered, "You would have no power over me if it were not given to you from above. Therefore, the one who handed me over to you is guilty of a greater sin."

Nathaniel had said that we were all responsible for the crucifixion of Jesus. We were all guilty of this great sin.

From then on, Pilate tried to set Jesus free, but the Jews kept shouting, "If you let this man go, you are no friend of Caesar. Anyone who claims to be a king opposes Caesar." When Pilate heard this, he brought Jesus out and sat down on the judge's seat at a place known as the Stone Pavement. It was the day of Preparation of Passover Week, about the sixth hour. "Here is your king," Pilate said to the Jews. But they shouted, "Take him away! Take him away! Crucify him!" "Shall I crucify your king?" Pilate asked. "We have no king but Caesar," the chief priests answered.

I thought the Jews' king was God, God was trying to give them a king and they rejected him. Just like I've rejected him.

Finally, Pilate handed him over to them to be crucified. So, the soldiers took charge of Jesus. Carrying his own cross, he went out to the place of the Skull (which in Aramaic is called Golgotha). Here they crucified him, and with him two others-one on each side and Jesus in the middle. Pilate had a notice prepared and fastened to the cross. It read: JESUS OF NAZARETH, THE KING OF THE JEWS. Many of the Jews read this sign, for the place where Jesus was crucified was near the city, and the sign was written in Aramaic, Latin and Greek. The chief priests of the Jews protested to Pilate, "Do not write 'The

King of the Jews,' but that this man claimed to be king of the Jews." Pilate answered, "What I have written, I have written." When the soldiers crucified Jesus, they took his clothes, dividing them into four shares, one for each of them, with the undergarment remaining. This garment was seamless, woven in one piece from top to bottom. "Let's not tear it," they said to one another. "Let's decide by lot who will get it." This happened that the scripture might be fulfilled which said, "They divided my garments among them and cast lots for my clothing." So, this is what the soldiers did. Near the cross of Jesus stood his mother, his mother's sister, Mary the wife of Clopas, and Mary Magdalene. When Jesus saw his mother there, and the disciple whom he loved standing nearby, he said to his mother, "Dear woman, here is your son," and to the disciple, "Here is your mother." From that time on, this disciple took her into his home. Later, knowing that all was now completed, and so that the Scripture would be fulfilled, Jesus said, "I am thirsty." A jar of wine vinegar was there, so they soaked a sponge in it, put the sponge on a stalk of the hyssop plant, and lifted it to Jesus' lips. When he had received the drink, Jesus said, "It is finished." With that, he bowed his head and gave up his spirit.

It was finished. He had paid with his life an atonement that I hadn't accepted. I wanted to but I couldn't let go, I wanted to let go. I had to let go.

"Naomi, are you okay?" Nathaniel said looking at me.

"Yes." I said quietly.

Lorna came out of the kitchen, "What's wrong? You're shaking."

I stared at her. "Why did he let it happen to me?" was all I could whisper.

"What happened to you?" Lorna said gently, the space between her eyebrows creasing.

I opened my mouth, but the words didn't come. I walked shakily to my violin and played, my eyes tightly closed. Memories flooded my mind, making me weak. Sparking jewels, silence, and cold. I shook as I felt his cold hands, and the tears that escaped from my eyes seared my cheeks as I continued to play. The world was spinning, and I continued playing. Opening my eyes, I could see Lorna through a river of tears.

"I'm so sorry, Naomi, I'm so sorry." She held me that night as he began to melt the thing that had gripped my soul for so long.

3 IT IS FINISHED

"Saturday's the big day."

"Yup, gradation."

Nathaniel and I sat across from each other at the Riviera. So many things had changed since my conversion, Lisa had left the Riviera to go to design school, church was actually exciting now, Nathaniel and I ate lunch every day, and now he was getting his Bachelors.

"So next you're going to get your master's?"

"Yeah, what about you? You ever thought about going to college?"

"Yeah I did," I smiled at him. "I would have never imagined in my wildest dreams that I would be where I am today."

"Yeah," He held his head in his hands, "So much has changed. It seems like yesterday that I made the decision to go to seminary."

"Yeah, a lot has changed."

He turned to look at me and the light coming in from the glass wall of the restaurant turned his eyes a honey brown.

"You're so different. I'm actually having lunch with someone who used to hate my guts. I always knew it would happen."

"What would happen?"

"That you would surrender your heart to God."

"You were always too confident." I said jokingly.

"It's faith."

I smiled and looked up at him. "Did you pray for me?" He smiled bright now. "Every day."

The line of black robes marched through the building. Excited family and friends filled the auditorium.

"Joshua Beals"

"Nathaniel Bennett"

Nathaniel walked across the stage and collected his diploma, his cheeks caving in as he smiled from ear to ear. Lorna took pictures wildly and all I could do was sit and stare. I was happy for him, I was. I remembered all of the colleges I applied to Princeton, Yale, Dartmouth, NYU, with majors ranging from business to pre-med. I never wanted to be a socialite who went to dinner parties to brag about how much money they made or their alma mater; that's what my mother wanted. An explosion of black hats flooded the auditorium and a tear escaped me.

"What's wrong Naomi?" Lorna said beside me as she continued to take pictures.

"Je le veux." I said, knowing she wouldn't understand.

One full year. The anniversary of my move to the city.

"So, everything is set Naomi, you'll be at Princeton in a few days. It's close enough to home so that you can come back if you need anything."

My mother looked at me from across the dinner table. I shoved a piece of food in mouth.

"Yup, I'll be gone."

"Sam, can you believe it's been a full year since I've been working here!" I said while he was doing his morning rounds.

"Yeah, you trying to get a raise?" He looked at me with a smirk on his face. "It won't happen."

"Peut-être" I teased.

"I remember that some sad looking teenager comes in here demanding that I give her a job. That's what I remember."

"First of all, I was never sad looking. And second, I got the job, didn't I?"

"By the skin of your teeth."

I sucked in a deep breath. "Sam," I hesitated, weighing my words. "I ran away from home, gave up my spot at Princeton."

He turned to face me completely now.

"There was just a lot going on and I had to leave. I was staying with a friend for a while and then things didn't work out..."

"Where do you live now?" Genuine concern filled his face.

"A woman from church, the preacher that eats lunch with me every day, that's her son."

"Oh, your boyfriend."

I blushed. "Sam, he's not my boyfriend."

"Yeah, sure he isn't." He said while he took a seat in front of me.

"Anyway, I want to thank you for everything that you've done. I don't know what this journey would be like if you weren't a part of it."

"You're a good kid, like the daughter I never had."

I smiled.

"Hey Naomi, I brought something home for you." Lorna called to me as she entered the house.

"What is it?"

She handed a packet in my hands. The Julliard School.

"An application?" I said lifting my eyebrows.

"Naomi, you can't bury the gifts God gives."

"I'm not burying them, I play every day at the Riviera, I sometimes play at church."

"I know you want to go to college. So, what's stopping you?"

There was no use in lying and telling her I didn't want to go, she would see right through that.

"I don't have the money to go to Julliard; I would need money from them to be able to go."

"Who?"

"My mom and my stepdad and I don't want anything from them, least of all money. That's what's stopping me." Lorna nodded her head in understanding. She was the only one who knew about my past.

"My husband had saved up money for my daughter to attend Julliard."

"I can't ask you to do that." I said sharply.

"I want to do this. I want you to go to school."

I leaned my hands on the kitchen counter to brace myself. I couldn't believe what I was hearing. I was starting to understand that there were no coincidences and that providence was the only thing that made sense for the things happening in my life.

"You'll help me get ready for the audition?" I asked her.

"I'll help you with anything you need."

"It says here that I have to get letters of recommendation and my high school transcript."

"Can you make a call?"

"No, we have to go and get it."

"All right so we'll go tomorrow."

The car ride to Long Island felt like it took forever. The traffic was terrible, and the long ride made it even worse for my nerves.

"Anxious?" Lorna asked, looking sideways at me.

"Do I look anxious?"

"Well you've been tapping on the glass for about twenty minutes."

"I didn't exactly plan on going back home."

"Well sometimes things don't go exactly as we plan. Maybe it would be good to go home to see things that you're familiar with. Maybe you'll even see some old friends."

"I didn't exactly have friends back home."

"Why not?"

"I just wasn't into the same things they were. They wanted to shop, and the others were so concentrated on being billionaires by the time they were thirty."

"Have you given some thought to visiting your parents?" She said looking over at me.

"Nope."

"Well maybe they'll come find you."

"I doubt it."

"Well, God constantly surprises you."

"I hope that's one surprise I hope he'll spare me."

Over the next few days I practiced, and Nathaniel filmed me playing a 19th century concerto in fast and slow movement, Bach's Sonata No.1 in G Minor in the Siciliano movement, and Paganini's 21st Caprice, Amoroso. I had to film myself and send it in, if they liked me they would request for a live audition in March. Later, Lorna made steaks for dinner and insisted that we all sit together at the dining table.

"I hope they'll request for me."

"They will." Nathaniel said.

"I hope so."

"They will."

"Does it ever bother you that I want to go to Julliard?" Nathaniel and I were watching TV.

"No," He looked at me strangely, "Why should it?"

"I mean, your sister wanted to go there, and she never got to."

"I'm happy that you'll get to go."

"I haven't even been called back for a live audition yet."

"You will," he said sounding exhausted.

"Always too confident."

"Always too doubtful." A smile played on his lips.

There was silence for a few minutes. "How did you forgive him?" I said abruptly.

"Forgive who?"

"The drunk driver. How'd you do it?"

He smiled and faced me.

"Well it's a little thing I'd like to call the Acts of Forgiveness. If you have $19.95 I could tell it to you."

I laughed. "What if I made a sandwich? Would that suffice?"

"Since, I like you so much, the sandwich will do."

We both laughed as we made our way to the kitchen. I began to make him a turkey sandwich as he spoke.

"Well, first I started to acknowledge him."

"What does that mean?"

"Instead of referring to him as the drunk driver, or other names I had for him, I started to call him by his name, it made him a person."

"And what was his name."

"Luke Tucker."

"And what did you do next?" I said handing him his sandwich.

"Thanks, "He said taking a bite. "You make really good sandwiches."

"Thank you, it's a specialty of mine."

"Anyway, well after I had mastered that, I started to pray that God would help me forgive him, help me see things from the driver's side."

"And what did he show you?"

"A man that needed a lot of help. A man that had been through a lot."

"So, what did you do next?" I said impatiently.

"Sorry, two steps a day. Maybe when you make me another sandwich I'll tell you the rest."

"That's cold."

"No, that's business."

I prayed every night to be able to forgive him. I prayed so hard. But I couldn't, I just couldn't.

"So, how's school?" I asked Nathaniel. We were having lunch again at the Riviera.

"Good. Letter still hasn't arrived?"

"Nope. It should be here in February."

"You don't mind if I ask you a personal question?"

"It depends."

"You never talk about your family. Um…I just wanted to know-

I couldn't avoid him now.

"My family lives in Westchester County."

"Westchester County? So, they have money?"

"Yeah, lots of it. My stepfather...um...
Travis," saying his name felt like swallowing acid. I
continued "He was a businessman."

"So, why'd you run away from home?"

"Well I was supposed to go Princeton, so
technically they knew I was leaving."

"They just didn't know where to."

"Exactly."

"Have you ever talked to them since you
left?"

"No."

"Do you plan to?"

"Honestly, no."

"Have they tried to make contact?"

"When I left I sort of threw my SIM card in a
lake." He burst out laughing. "You didn't!"

"I did." I took a sip of my soda. "If they
wanted to really find me, they would have." I
continued drinking.

He looked at me for a long time and took a
deep breath. "So, I return to my question. Why'd you
leave?"

I shrugged. Should I tell him? I knew I
wouldn't.

"I don't know, I just couldn't stay."

"School is great! My portfolio is coming along, but it's
a lot of work." Lisa and I talked on the phone every
once in a while.

"Maybe you can design a dress for me someday."

"That's a great idea!" Lisa started to speak a mile a minute the ideas forming in her mind. "You would look great in yellow, not too bright because then-"

"Lisa, slow down, it was just a suggestion."

"Thanks for breaking my heart." She said sarcastically.

I laughed. "But there is something you can do for me. Well it's more for you but-"

"What is it?"

"Will you come to church with me on Sunday?"

"Church?"

"Yeah church, you could bring your boyfriend. I've been trying to get Sam to come and he finally agreed just because last week was my birthday."

There was a long silence.

"Are you there?"

"Yeah," She sounded unsure. She wasn't going to come. "Yeah I'll come, just give me the address."

I was excited as I dressed for church. What if Sam or Lisa got saved today? I had already given Nathaniel a heads up that they were coming. I hoped he preached a message on salvation today. We pulled up to the church and I saw Lisa and Sam talking outside.

"You came."

"We told you we'd come." Lisa said shivering in the cold. "Sorry Jay couldn't make it."

"That's okay, at least you're here," The wind howled. "Let's go inside." The service was good as usual. Nathaniel preached on righteousness.

"But we are all like an unclean thing,
And all our righteousness is as filthy rags;
We all fade as a leaf,
And our iniquities, like the wind,
Have taken us away."

I constantly looked over at Sam and Lisa seeing if they were bored, interested, even captivated. But I couldn't read their faces. Lord please help them to know you. I would be patient just like Lorna and Nathaniel. When church was over Sam quickly left saying he needed to get to the restaurant. Lisa stood outside with me.

"Church was nice."

"Yeah, it was."

"I've never heard Nathaniel preach, I bet you enjoy that every week."

I smiled. "It's not like that."

"Why not?"

"Come on you can't be serious? He's not even interested."

"You never know, he might be. But you are, aren't you?"

I shook my head in frustration. "Does it even matter?"

Lisa looked at me incredulously. "Of course it matters! It makes all the difference in the world."

"He's a preacher, he was raised in the church, and my life is so different."

"That doesn't matter. You guys have similar lives now. You past doesn't have to dictate how you live your life."

"But it usually does."

"I think that's a choice you're making."

I didn't know how to answer her.

"Okay I'm ready." Lorna sat on the couch ready to play our game again. I picked up my violin and began to play. I let my mind run wild, trying to trip her up, even if it was one time. What if Lisa was right? What if I didn't get into Julliard/ What would I do then? I couldn't live with Lorna forever; she might get tired of me.

"Worry." Lorna blurted out. "You're worried about something."

"This is unnatural." I said laughing.

She laughed but soon turned serious. "What are you worried about?"

"Julliard." That was partly true.

"Don't worry Naomi, you'll get in. God has a plan for you and I know Julliard is a part of it."

I nodded absentmindedly.

"That's not all, is it?"

"It's nothing. I don't even know why it's on my mind."

"So, what is it?"

I couldn't tell Lorna. It was...well...embarrassing. "If I promise that I won't let it bother me anymore, will I have to tell?"

"Only if you keep the promise."

"All right, I promise."

My eyes watered, and my lip burst from the weather today. I quickly headed home so that I could enjoy the benefits of a heater. As soon as I opened the door Lorna rushed at me.

"It's here! It came in the mail today and I had to stop myself from opening it!"

"The letter, it's here!"

"Open it! Come on!" She pushed the letter into my hands.

"I don't know. I'm too nervous."

"You better open that letter before I do."

I took a deep breath and slid my finger into the opening of the envelope. I slowly opened it my hands shaking.

"To Miss. Naomi Beckford, We request your presence at the live auditions for The Julliard School."

I screamed, "They want me to do the live audition."

Lorna hugged and squeezed me tight. "I knew, I knew it! I'm going to call Nathaniel and tell him."

While Lorna ran to the phone I contemplated on the last year. I went from leaving my parents' home with no money, no job, no family or friends. Now I had everything I needed and more. God had changed my life so radically.

"Bye Naomi, I'll see you later." She was right all along.

"Sam, what will happen if I leave? I mean if I get into Julliard?" I was shining the glasses and Sam was making his morning rounds.

"I don't know Naomi, I'll miss you, but this is a good thing. You're going to school, I always thought that you belonged in a prestigious college rather than being a waitress."

"I was pretty good at being a waitress." I teased.

His golden eyes lit as he smiled. "Yeah after the first month you got much better. I thought I was gonna have to fire you."

I laughed. "You didn't though."

"Yeah, well, I might just change my mind. You're still working here until August."

I sat at the counter resting my chin in my hands. "So much has changed and so much is going to continue to change. It's like I never know what's in store for me."

"That's the beauty of life. It's a part of the journey."

"I wonder what this journey has in store for me."

"You'll find out, you just have to keep breathing."

"If you could do anything in this world, what would you do?"

He looked down at the food he was preparing in deep concentration. "I don't know. I never really thought about it." He chopped at some tomatoes. "What would you do?"

"Forget."

Today's weather was horrible. It was about twenty degrees making it difficult to breathe. The cold seeped in my bones making me feel as though I couldn't move. I told Lorna I was going to take a walk today. I didn't even know where I was going. Maybe it was anxiety over my upcoming audition or the fact that I hated being stuck in a house for so long, but here I was breathing in ice on a Saturday afternoon. I had never taken notice of the places close to the house; my days consisted of work, school, and church. I walked to a bench that was on the outskirts of a playground and rested. Close by a family with their kids were having a snowball fight. What was my mother doing now? Did she look different? What story did she and Travis concoct to explain to their friends why I never came back? I had never worried about this, never even given it a second thought. What if I went home to see them? No, I wouldn't, I couldn't. I left my mother and Travis in the past and that's where they were going to stay. In the past.

"Out of the depths have I cried unto thee, O LORD. Lord, hear my voice: let thine ears be attentive to the voice of my supplications. If thou, LORD, shouldest mark iniquities, O Lord, who shall stand? But there is forgiveness with thee, that thou mayest be feared. I wait for the LORD, my soul doth wait, and in his word do I hope. My soul waiteth for the Lord more than they that watch for the morning: I say, more than they that watch for the morning. Let Israel hope in the LORD: for with the LORD there is mercy, and with him is plenteous redemption. And he shall redeem Israel from all his iniquities."

"Where would we be without the grace and mercy of God?" Nathaniel was preaching this morning. "We would be a lost people, condemned to hell. But the Lord redeemed us, washed us in his blood, and snatched us from the hands of the enemy."

A chorus of amens and hallelujahs filled the sanctuary. "As the scripture says, if God should mark our iniquities, who could stand? God has stricken the record; God has thrown our sins into the sea of forgetfulness. Now what must we do to show our appreciation? Serve him, praise him, worship him, but we must share that same grace, that same mercy, our same hope with another. That's the heartbeat of the Christian faith. That's the heartbeat of Christ."

Today was the big day. I got no sleep last night; I took forty-five minutes in the shower trying to calm myself down and now I was fixing my hair for the fourth time. *Breathe, just breathe.* I smoothed my hands on the long, navy blue dress Lorna and I had picked out.

"Naomi, are you ready?" Lorna shouted from downstairs.

"Yes." I left the room and stepped downstairs where she and Nathaniel were waiting.

"How do I look?"

"You look so pretty," she said pulling my arms. "But we have to go. So, come on!"

All of us rushed out of the house to the car. The ride to Julliard was quiet. Lorna looked outside the window the entire time and Nathaniel stared straight ahead, and his knuckles tightly gripped the steering wheel. What could I say? Nathaniel and Lorna were passing the place where Michelle and Rev. Bennet died. I looked out the window trying to figure out where it might have happened. Was it at this four-way intersection or at the next one? I looked out windows watching the glass building come into view. Still silent, Nathaniel parked, and we exited the car. I approached the desk at the front.

"Hi, I'm here for an audition. Do you know where I go?"

"Music, Dance, or Drama?"

"Music."

"The green arrows will direct you. Good luck."

Lorna once told me that we didn't need luck, that God had everything planned. God showed favor, he didn't grant luck.

"I'm going to go to the bathroom. I'll be right back." Lorna quickly rushed to the bathroom.

"I'm really sorry." Nathaniel said.

"For what?"

"I know we haven't been really attentive. It's just that it's my first time driving over here, seeing where she died...."

"It's okay."

"My mom's a little emotional too," He smiled trying to lighten the mood. "I know you're going to do great. You're going to make it in."

"There goes that unwavering confidence."

"I wish you'd get rid of that relentless doubt."

I laughed nervously, rubbing my neck.

"Do you see what I'm talking about? Just relax."

"You're right," I said taking a deep breath. "I'm calm."

Lorna came out of the bathroom. "Before you register I just want you to know that not only are Nathaniel and I here, but God is here with you too. He'll make sure you don't miss a note and who knows he may even make the judges give you a standing ovation."

We all laughed, and Lorna kissed my cheek. "You're going to do perfect. Love you."

"Love you too."

We went to the registration desk. At least the girl at the desk looked friendly. She was probably a student.

"Musician or vocalist?

"Musician."

"What instrument?"

"Violin."

"Name?"

"Naomi Beckford."

"All right you can go to Paul Recital Hall."

"Thanks," I turned to Lorna and Nathaniel. "So, I'll see you guys later."

The wait in the auditorium consisted of me tapping my violin, fixing my bow, and watching amazing violinists.

"Beckford, Naomi."

I scrambled to my feet nearly tripping on my dress. "Yes, I'm here." I walked slowly to the stage.

Three teachers sat at a lighted table. I smiled at them trying to lighten the mood. No smile back.

"May we hear your Paganini caprice?

I started to play Paganini's 24th caprice. Lord please just help through this.

"Stop. Okay, play your Bach sonata."

I decided to play the same one I had done for my pre-screening audition, Bach's Sonata No.1 in G Minor in the Siciliano movement. This time again in about two minutes I was told to stop playing. They asked for my major and minor scales and arpeggios. I was pretty sure I aced that, but once again when I was asked to do my slow and fast movement of a 20th century piece I was stopped before I finished.

"Your twentieth century piece please."

They weren't going to stop me now. I had to play something that would make them listen. Something I could make an emotional connection with. I started to play the Second Gymnopédie. At first, I watched them, to see if they were paying attention, if they were moved. But soon, I closed my eyes letting the music wash over me. The only physical thing I was aware of was the up and down movements of my bow. Okay, Naomi, last note. I was able to finish.

"Thank you, Miss. Beckford." She smiled at me. I smiled in return breathing a sigh of relief. Thank you, Lord.

I exited the auditorium, my eyes roaming the building for any sign of Nathaniel or Lorna. They were at a nearby table. Lorna rushed over to me.

"So how did it go?"

"Great."

"I knew it would. So, let's go out to dinner somewhere to celebrate." God had taken care of me today, he had shown me favor. He always has.

I had made it in. I stared at the paper in utter shock. "We are pleased to inform you that you have been accepted into the Julliard School." I knew I hadn't done this on my own. God had intervened. God had Lorna bring me that application. God had put everything in order. Finally looking up, the expectant faces of Lorna and Nathaniel watched me.

"I got in." Lorna nearly had a heart attack. She jumped and screamed for sheer joy. Nathaniel let out a loud whoop and soon I was flooded by hugs from Lorna.

"I knew it. I just knew it. Thank you, Jesus. Thank you, Lord." Lorna wiped tears from her cheeks. "I'm gonna make a few phone calls, I have to tell everyone." She walked away to the kitchen.

"Congratulations." Nathaniel said.

"Thank you."

"I knew you'd make it."

"If I wasn't a Christian I might believe you were a fortune teller." He laughed and soon the air was filled with tension. He stayed silent, looking at me.

"What?" I said softly.

"I don't exactly know how to say this."

"Say what?" He never looked nervous before.

"Um," he loudly drew in a breath of air and looked up at me. "Would you like to go out to dinner on Saturday? I mean it would be celebrating your acceptance."

"Dinner?"

"Yeah."

"Just the two of us?"

"Yeah."

Nathaniel wanted to take me out…on a date. I would have never seen this coming. "I would like that."

On Friday Lisa decided we needed to go shopping for an outfit to wear on Saturday night. I didn't know exactly what to wear and asking Lorna to take me shopping for a date with her son was out of the question. My cheeks had flooded with heat of the embarrassment of having to tell her I was going out on a date with Nathaniel.

"That looks nice, but it's not the one." I had just finished trying on a pink dress. In the end, we decided on a white day dress with blue embroidery on the hem. As I looked at myself in the mirror it still shocked me that I was going out with Nathaniel tomorrow. I went from avoiding him to actually wanting to go out to dinner with him. He had been one of the key players in my process of becoming a Christian. He still played a vital role in my growth. He was a gentleman, a righteous man, and I couldn't have him. I was tainted. What would he say when he found out I wasn't a virgin? He probably had spent his whole life waiting for someone pure, someone untouched. Things between us would eventually go wrong and our relationship would cease to exist. And worse, the relationship I had with Lorna would suffer. I couldn't risk it. Things had worked out so well for me in these last two years. I couldn't let this ruin that.

I would go out with him tomorrow and tell him that it couldn't go any further, and he would move on and find someone else. Someone better than me.

To my dismay, Lisa showed up today to get me ready for my date.

"This isn't that big of a deal Lisa."

"Oh, yes, it is. I waited a year for him to ask you out and you're gonna look good." She curled my hair lightly and put it in a half up half down hairstyle. After, she decided that I needed a little makeup.

"I hate wearing makeup."

"I won't put a lot on. Besides, Nathaniel doesn't strike me as the kind of guy who likes a face full of makeup." She walked over to my jewelry box. "What do we have in here? Oh Naomi, this is perfect!" she said pulling out a pair of small flower shaped diamond stud earrings.

"Where did you get this?"

"My dad gave them to me before he died."

"You should wear them more often. They're so pretty." Finally, Lisa was done with all her beauty treatments.

"Oh, Naomi you look so pretty." Lorna said as I came downstairs.

"Thank you."

"Nathaniel should be here soon."

Nathaniel arrived five minutes early. My cheeks filled with heat when he said I looked beautiful in front of Lisa and Lorna. He took me to a Spanish restaurant called Madrid.

"This place is really nice."

"Well, I hope you didn't expect me to take you to McDonalds."

"Well, I was a little worried that you might." I joked. The food was great, and the conversation stayed light and fun. We talked about the church, his seminary, and Julliard.

"So, I never asked how it was to go back to Hewlett Bay."

"It was fine." I said coldly.

"Did you see any old friends or anything?"

"Nope. Just my music teacher."

"Don't you worry that word will get around to your parents that you were in town?"

"I don't care if it does."

"You said that you couldn't stay. Did they really hurt you that bad?" I hated when the conversation resorted to this. I didn't want to talk about them.

"Yes. Let's just say I live with what they did every day for the rest of my life. Does that define 'bad'?"

"You don't have to make it affect you every day or much worse for the rest of your life."

I stroked my forehead in frustration. He had a way of making me feel as though I was always two steps behind.

"You know what, I'm sorry about that. Do you mind if I show you something?"

"Sure."

He picked up the check and we drove on a familiar road. When we got close I realized where we were.

"Did anyone ever tell you taking your date to church is not exactly romantic?"

"Ha-ha, I just want you to know something."

He opened the door to the church and we walked the familiar way down the aisle. We walked all the way to the piano.

"When my dad and my sister died I was so angry. My mom had problems controlling me, I would lash out for no reason at all, and I started skipping school. Not even my mom knows this, but I even considered suicide." He walked over to the piano. "I bet you didn't know this, but I used to play piano. I never had the passion or the expertise like my sister, but we both started out playing together. When she died I stopped playing completely. At first my mom tried to get me to play, but I wouldn't; now she doesn't even mention it. Before you got here the piano at the house was just collecting dust." He cleared his throat. "And here I am telling you what to do about your family. All these years I tried to convince myself that I was over it, that I had let it go."

He sat down and slowly trailed his hands over the keys as if trying to register them all in his mind. Slowly he started to play a sweet song, it sounded mournful, but mesmerizing. I watched him intently. He closed his eyes and played. I slowly made my way to the piano, my eyes never leaving him. As if in slow motion, I sat next to him, watching his fingers on the piano. As I sat there, a sudden realization hit me. I couldn't let this be the last time I went out with him. I couldn't tell him that this was the furthest it could go. I was in love with Nathaniel Bennett.

The months flew by quicker than I would have imagined. I had prepared myself for school, stocking up on staff paper and other necessities. But today I felt gloomy, wandering around the house from lack of sleep. Today was my last day at the Riviera. I headed off to work, staring out the windows, looking at every face that I came into contact with, trying to remember every detail about this day. As usual, I helped Sam get the morning things ready and I stayed after and waited for everyone to leave.

"Two years." I said turning towards him.

"Yup, it seems like yesterday. I'm gonna miss you."

"We'll still see each other. Lorna says not to be alone for Thanksgiving. She says you know where to come."

He laughed. "Tell her I will definitely be there."

"I brought something for you. It's a bit of a going away present." I handed him a gift bag.

"It's not orthopedic shoes is it?" he joked.

I smiled. "No, I actually thought about it but I decided not to go for a comedic effect." As he opened it I continued. "It's a French bible, just like the one your mom used to read to you." He slowly turned it over in his hand examining it.

"It looks exactly like it." He said in disbelief. "Thank you."

"You're welcome."

"I have something for you too." He walked to the back of the restaurant and brought out a brand-new violin. "I figured a violinist can't just have one violin."

"I can't believe it!" I said stroking it.

"I wish you the best that life has to offer. You deserve the best of everything and I hope you always strive for that."

"I will."

"You asked me a long time ago that if I had the power to do anything, what I would do? I didn't know back then. But, I decided I'd get whatever you got."

"Well, that's easy. He's in your gift."

Sam had started coming to church every week with us. He hadn't gotten saved, but I was praying every day for him and Lisa. I went to school Monday through Friday and endured grueling training on my violin. I took composition, theory, ear training and performance classes. Violin majors were required to perform in an orchestra depending on an audition. I was chosen for the New Julliard Ensemble which played music from the post-WWII era. I also played in the Julliard Orchestra, which is required from all musicians. I had already played in two shows, everyone including Sam and Lisa were there. We had played Holzt's The Planets for the orchestra and the soundtrack from Atonement for the ensemble. This Christmas season the orchestra was to accompany the dance department in The Sleeping Beauty ballet. Thanksgiving was next week, and Lorna sent Nathaniel and I out to the supermarket with a huge grocery list.

"Geez, how many people is my mom cooking for this year?" Nathaniel said as he pushed the shopping cart through the aisle.

"I don't know, it seems like half of New York City can come over."

"Well, at least the food will be good. And I'll get to spend a little more time with you." He took my hand in his. "We've both been so busy."

"Yeah, I know. Why don't we go for lunch tomorrow?"

"That sounds good." He raised my hand to his lips and softly kissed it.

One thing I loved about him was that he never pushed any boundaries. We had never kissed; holding hands and light pecks on the cheek was the farthest we had gone. I could tell it wasn't that he didn't want to go farther, but I think he was always gauging my readiness. I liked the ease I felt around him, he was the first man to treat me with respect. Everyone always had an agenda that ended in sex. There were times that I'd just watch him when he wasn't aware and think that I didn't deserve him. Someone this patient, this loving. I never told him my past and I knew at some point it would have to come up. Just not today.

"Lord we thank you for this food that we are about to eat. We thank you for allowing us to see another year in perfect health and in perfect peace. We pray that you'll bless this food and bless everyone who will partake of this food, in Jesus name we pray, Amen." Our hands unclasped and

4

everyone reached for their favorite dish. Lorna sat at the head of the table smiling as everyone dug into the food. Sam shared himself polite helpings and Nathaniel shared himself a hefty portion of sweet yams. Jackie, a girl about my age from church also put moderate portions on her plate probably in an attempt not to look too greedy in front of the first family. Lorna raised her glass and fork and made a few dings.

"I want us to go around the table and say what we are truly thankful for this year. I'll start, I'm thankful for this year of blessings on which God has bestowed upon me. I have never been in need or want. He has blessed me so that I could be a blessing to others. He has been my Jehovah Jireh, more than enough."

"I thank God for letting me see another year in perfect health." Jackie said. Sam was next. "I thank God for giving me understanding."

"I thank God for drawing me closer to him and for giving me the desire of my heart." My turn. Everyone looked at me. "I thank God for being my father."

Twenty-one. I had lived to see twenty-one. God had been patient with me. For nineteen years I had rejected him, and he never left, never stopped knocking at my heart. How would my life have been without him? What course would I have taken? Living without him was not an option anymore. Turning back was impossible. I had to run this race and finish strong, I had to see my father, my high priest.

"I love you, Lord." I prayed. "I love you so much." When I got downstairs, Lorna cooked me my favorite breakfast; French toast, bacon and scrambled eggs, with strawberries on the side. Nathaniel surprised me by coming to my school to take me out for lunch.

"Are you starting to feel old?" Nathaniel joked. "No," I said. If I'm old, then you're ancient." He smiled, his dimples making indents on his face.

"Twenty- three isn't so bad."

"Well, twenty-one has its perks as well."

"No drinking, Naomi." He said sarcastically.

"Ha-ha."

"Do you remember the missions trip that my school is taking to Haiti?"

"Yeah."

"Well, I got accepted into the program. All expenses paid, it would count towards my doctorate."

"That's great!" I kissed his cheek. "So, when do you go?"

"I'm not sure if I'll go."

"What do mean you're not sure?"

"The trip is for two years."

"Two years?"

"Yeah."

Two years without Nathaniel, it was hard to imagine. "I still think you should go. You shouldn't waste an opportunity like this. This is what you've wanted for so long."

"I know, I guess I have some praying to do."

"I guess so."

"I tell you the truth; no one can see the kingdom of God unless he is born again." Today Rev. Jones preached, and Sam sat next to me his knuckles tightly gripping his bible. "I tell you the truth; no one can enter the kingdom of God unless he is born of water and the Spirit. Flesh gives birth to flesh, but the Spirit gives birth to spirit. You should not be surprised at my saying, 'You must be born again.' The wind blows wherever it pleases. You hear its sound, but you cannot tell where it comes from or where it is going. So, it is with everyone born of the Spirit." His knuckles were now white. "For God so loved the world that he gave his one and only Son, that whoever believes in him shall not perish but have eternal life. For God did not send his Son into the world to condemn the world, but that through him the world would be saved." Tears ran down his cheeks and he got up leaving the church. I walked outside into the icy weather after him, trying not to make a scene.

"Please Sam, don't leave." He stopped walking, but he didn't turn around to face me. "It had that same effect on me too. It's like a mirror to your soul, showing you everything you're not. Am I right?" He still didn't say anything, and I walked closer to him. "He's calling you, you can hear him, don't turn him away."

He turned around now facing me. "What if I can't be everything he wants me to be? What happens when I keep on messing up? Will he still love me?"

I stepped closer now and held his hand in mine. "For I am persuaded, that neither death, nor life, nor angels, nor principalities, nor powers, nor things present, nor things to come, nor height, nor depth, nor any other creature, shall be able to separate us from the love of God, which is in Christ Jesus our Lord."

He wept bitterly now. "I'm so sorry for everything I've done. I'm so sorry, so sorry."

"He knows, and he forgives you Sam. He forgives you." And Sam was saved on the 28th of January in the parking lot of the church. I wondered how the Lord would write that down in his Book of Life.

"What are you doing here?" Nathaniel stood outside my last class for the day.

"I thought you might want to have some fun."

"What kind of fun?"

"You'll see."

Nathaniel took me to Rye Playland. I had never had so much fun in my life. We went on every ride in the park.

"This was awesome." I said eating an ice cream cone.

"I was hoping you'd have fun. Sometimes you need to take a break from your schedule."

"You're right, I needed this."

We walked in silence for a few moments.

"So, have you turned in your stuff for your trip?"

"Not yet."

"When's the deadline?"

"June 12th."

"It's the 20th! What are you waiting for?"

"A confirmation."

"A confirmation of what?

"I just can't do it until I know something first."

"And what might that be?"

"Don't worry about it."

"I hate it when you keep secrets from me."

"I know," he said taking a sip of soda. "But this is a good secret, I promise."

Rev. Jones was preaching this morning from Philippians 4:8 "Finally, brothers, whatever is true, whatever is noble, whatever is right, whatever is pure, whatever is lovely, whatever is admirable-if anything is excellent or praiseworthy-think about such things. Whatever you have learned or received or heard from me, or seen in me-put it into practice. And the God of peace will be with you." I rose up from my seat and went to the bathroom. I entered the stall and I could hear the whooshing sound of the door.

"Yeah, I definitely think something is going on between them."

"...And with her living at Sis. Lorna's house, you can only imagine what else is going on." Jackie's voice. My breath caught, and the room seemed to spin.

"I don't think they're having sex or anything, Rev. Nathaniel seems too good for that. But then again, she did say in small group one time that she had a bad life back home. Why would he want something like that?"

"Which is exactly my point. She has to be giving him something for him to want her."

"Come on we have to head back out before they come in for us." I heard the whooshing sound of the door and I stood there and cried in the stall for the rest of the service.

"What's wrong you haven't been yourself lately?" Lorna sat on the couch watching TV.

"Nothing."

"Well it doesn't seem like nothing."

"Just a few rough days at school." *Liar.*

"Naomi, I know you better than that. Every day at school is tough."

"I just don't want to talk about it."

"Okay, I won't push," she said shaking her head. "But you know I'm here to listen."

"Yeah I know."

I left and headed for school. During my performance class I felt a vibration in my pocket. A text from Lorna. GO TO LISA'S AFTER SCHOOL. Lisa's apartment? Why would Lorna want me to go to Lisa's house? I sent a text back, WHY?

JUST GO. After school I took the train to Lisa's apartment.

"Hey you're here."

"Yeah, why did Lorna tell me to come here?"

"Because I'm gonna get you ready."

"Ready for what?"

"I'm not at liberty to speak."

Lisa did my hair and makeup. "Come on you have to tell me. What's the occasion?"

"Sorry I can't say, I promised. Hold on, I have one more thing." She ran off into another room and came back with a black evening gown.

"This is for you. Put it on."

"You bought this?"

"I made it. You like it?"

"I love it." I said running my hands over it. "You have to tell me what I'm getting dressed up for."

"I wish I could tell you and if you keep pressuring me I might squeal so just put on the dress and these shoes," she handed me a matching pair of heels, "and go downstairs."

"What's downstairs?"

"A limo to take you to your destination."

"A limo!"

"Yeah, a limo." she said shooing me. "Hurry up and get dressed. You don't want to keep the driver waiting all night."

Lisa helped me into my dress and I ran downstairs to the limo. Why would Lorna send me to Lisa's apartment to get all made up and send me in a limousine?

"Driver, do you know where I'm going?"

"Yes."

"Would you mind telling me?"

"Sorry, I've been given strict orders not to say a word." So, the driver was in on it too. Where was I going? I sat back and stared out the window hoping to catch a familiar route. Soon I realized I knew this route too well. No, it couldn't be. Why would a limo take me there? The stop the driver made in front of the church confirmed my thoughts.

"Why did you drop me off at my church?"

The driver shrugged. "Just following orders."

I slowly walked inside. A piano played a lovely melody. I walked the aisle looking for the person on the piano, but they were hidden. I walked up more. Nathaniel. His eyes watched me, and he smiled, his dimples showing.

"So, you're behind this?"

"It would seem so." He said still playing.

I walked closer now. "What song is that?"

"My sister composed it."

"It's beautiful."

He continued to play, still looking at me. "You're beautiful." He finished playing and got up from the piano, dressed in a fully tailored black suit. "For years I prayed for God to show me my wife. And he did. Then I asked for him to send her to me. And I saw you that day in the Riviera. You are everything I asked for and more. "

I closed my eyes, breathing deeply. Is this really happening? *Breathe Naomi, breathe.*

"I love you and I want to marry you. I want to be able to grow old with you. I want to see your face every morning when I wake up." He stood in front of me now holding my hand. "Marry me?" he said getting on one knee.

I stared down at him unable to speak. *Say something!*

"Naomi." I still looked down at him, frozen. "I can't."

A mix of shock and sadness filled his face. He swallowed down hard. "You can't?"

"I'm sorry." I backed away from him. "I'm so sorry."

He nodded his head and rose up. "I'm sorry too." We looked at each other for a few moments before I turned and ran out of the church.

I had never talked to Lorna about that night. We acted as though it had never happened. She never talked about it; probably in an attempt not to embarrass or upset me. Nathaniel had registered for the two-year missions trip to Haiti shortly after that night. We still saw each other often, even though he didn't come by the house as often. We were cordial towards one another, greeting each other in friendly tones. But I could see the hurt in his eyes. I had put it there, I had spurned him, I had broken his heart. He decided not to attend his graduation for his master's degree, so Lorna decided to have a family dinner. The dinner conversation was tense and consisted of mainly Lorna and Nathaniel talking, I had removed myself from the conversation.

"May I please be excused?"

"Sure." Lorna said

I put my plate and glass in the sink and went to my room. There was a knock at my door. I opened it and Nathaniel stood there, his eyes looking into mine.

"I just wanted to talk to you."

"Yeah, sure."

"I just came to tell you that I'm leaving on Saturday."

Saturday. Today was Thursday. He would leave, and I wouldn't see him again for two years. "I hope you have a good time."

He hung his head and bit his lip. "That's it? 'I hope you have a good time.'" He stared at me waiting for me to respond.

"I don't know what you want me to say."

He searched my eyes. "Nothing. I don't want you to say anything." He turned and left me clutching the doorway for the support I needed.

He was leaving today. Lorna had already left to drop him at the airport. I needed a hot shower. I got in the tub and turned on the faucet, letting the hot water run over my skin. *He's gone.* My hands trembled. *You let him get away.* I made the water hotter. *He's gone.* I brought my hands to my mouth suppressing my bitter cries.

After Nathaniel left I completely immersed myself into my music. I composed twenty pieces in a year. I constantly played my violin or the piano. I got high marks and praises from my teachers and was even given an opportunity to take a master class with Itzhak Perlman. At home when I wasn't playing the violin I simply stayed in my room watching TV. Lorna and I still talked but the conversations were one-dimensional. I could see Lorna's looks of worry whenever she listened to my music. She never commented on what they were about, but I could tell she knew. I didn't know how to talk to her about this. I prayed but to no avail. I read the Bible but couldn't find any answers. Nathaniel sent letters and emails updating us on how he was doing, but I couldn't bring myself to ever respond. Lorna usually wrote and told him I said hi. Today I stayed in my room working on a sonata. A knock at my door broke my concentration.

Lorna opened the door and stepped in the room closing the door behind her. "We need to talk."

"About what?"

"You know what it's about Naomi." I just stared at her. "Ever since Nathaniel left, it's like you've gone into some mode of depression. All you do is play your violin and the piano all day, you don't smile, you don't do anything. You can't do this to yourself."

"You think I want to be like this?"

"Then why didn't you say yes?"

"I couldn't."

"Couldn't or wouldn't?"

I gazed at her for a few moments before responding.

"Nathaniel and I are like oil and water we just wouldn't mix."

"You two seemed to be mixing pretty well for three years."

"You don't understand."

"Make me understand."

"He comes from a godly home and I come from home filled with sex and drugs." Hot tears spilled down my cheeks. "What would he say when he found out that I wasn't a virgin? That I was raped by my stepfather for four years. What would he say?" I wiped the tears from my cheeks. "He deserves better than me."

"So that's what it comes down to, your stepfather." She moved closer to me. "Listen to me, what your stepfather did was horrible, a disgusting act. But you have the power to change your circumstances. Forgiveness is a hard concept for all of us to grasp Naomi. Remember that the same mercy that you refuse to give to your parents is the same mercy God will withhold from you. "

"I don't know how to forgive them."

"Yes, you do. Now it's time to just do it."

"Our Father which art in heaven, Hallowed be thy name. Thy kingdom come. Thy will be done in earth, as it is in heaven. Give us this day our daily bread. And forgive us our debts, as we forgive our debtors. And lead us not into temptation, but deliver us from evil: For thine is the kingdom, and the power, and the glory, forever. Amen."

I didn't understand. I had looked up every scripture about forgiveness. All of them told me to forgive but didn't show me how to forgive. *Father please guide me.*

Lorna and I sat on the couch watching TV. It was too cold to go outside for anything. The phone rang.

"I'll get it." I picked up the phone.

"Hi, is a Miss. Naomi Beckford there?"

"Yes, this is she. May I ask who's calling?"

"It's your mother."

I froze. "I'm sorry, who did you say you were?"

"It's me Naomi."

"Who is it?" Lorna asked. I didn't answer.

"How did you get this number?" I said coldly.

"Sweetheart we always knew where you were, we didn't even need a private investigator to figure that out."

"What do you want?"

"I just called to see if you would come home, even if it's just for a visit."

"No."

"Please Naomi, Travis is sick. I need you."

"Where were you when I needed you?" I said through my teeth.

"That's in the past. Just come home."

"No, you're in my past." I said as I hung up.

I rose up from the couch, rubbing my temples. "Who was that?" Lorna said.

"My mother."

"What happened?" Lorna said coming off the couch to stand next to me.

"She wants me to come home. Travis is sick."

Lorna looked at me and didn't speak for a while. "What are you going to do?"

"Nothing, let her deal with her sick husband." Bitterness oozed from my words.

"Naomi, you can't do that."

"Yes, I can. At least if he dies, then he can't do it to another person." My voice rose in anger, "What if I'm not the only one? At least God decided to be fair this time, Travis pays for what he did."

Lorna watched me and didn't say a word. The silence calmed me. "I'm ashamed of you, Naomi." She stepped closer to me, cupping my face in her hands. "If I speak in the tongues of men and of angels, but have not love, I am only a resounding gong or a clanging cymbal. That's what you sound like now, just a clanging cymbal."

She went upstairs to her room. Love them? They never loved me. *I loved you first.* "Lord it's too hard to love them."

I never give you more than you can bear. My grace is sufficient.

"Show me how to love them, show me how." I walked over to the bible on top of the piano and looked down. It was opened to the concordance. I trailed my finger down. LOVE. 1 Corinthians 13. I turned the pages to it.

"If I speak in the tongues of men and of angels, but have not love, I am only a resounding gong or a clanging cymbal. If I have the gift of prophecy and can fathom all mysteries and all knowledge, and if I have a faith that can move mountains, but have not love, I am nothing. If I give all I possess to the poor and surrender my body to the flames, but have not love, I gain nothing.

Love is patient, love is kind. It does not envy, it does not boast, it is not proud. It is not rude, it is not self-seeking, it is not easily angered, it keeps no record of wrongs. Love does not delight in evil but rejoices with the truth. It always protects, always trusts, always hopes, always perseveres.

Love never fails. But where there are prophecies, they will cease; where there are tongues, they will be stilled; where there is knowledge, it will pass away. For we know in part and we prophesy in part, but when perfection comes, the imperfect disappears. When I was a child, I talked like a child, I thought like a child, I reasoned like a child. When I became a man, I put childish ways behind me. Now we see but a poor reflection as in a mirror; then we shall see face to face. Now I know in part; then I shall know fully, even as I am fully known.

And now these three remain: faith, hope and love. But the greatest of these is love. *My grace is sufficient Naomi; my strength is made perfect in your weakness.*

Every day when I woke up I read 1 Corinthians 13. Every day I was determined to apply this to my life. I was out of school for the summer and I wasn't exactly the type to stay at home and watch TV all day. I grabbed my phone and called Lisa.

"Hey, I was wondering if you wanted to have lunch with me today? My treat."

"Really? Sure."

"Okay, meet me at the Riviera at 12:00."

Lisa and I laughed all through lunch, reminiscing about the days where we worked here. Sam joined in the conversation once in a while, laughing about my clumsiness and Lisa's aversion to selling anyone snails and caviar.

"We had good times here, didn't we?" Lisa said smiling.

"Yeah we did."

"You know, I broke up with Jay." Lisa said abruptly

"You did?"

"He moved out last night. You were right. I deserve better than some musician who's an alcoholic." She looked out the window and quickly wiped a tear from her eye. "I'm sorry, I just need some time to get over it."

"No, take your time. I'll be here through it all."

She looked at me and smiled. "Thank you." I spent two days sleeping over Lisa's house consoling her. She cried every night.

"Do you ever think I'll get over it?"

"You will. It'll just take some time."

"Miss. Beckford may I please see you after class." My violin instructor called to me. *Oh no, what did I do?* The rest of the class my heart thumped wildly within me and my palms started to sweat.

"Yes, Mrs. Reiser, you wanted to see me."

"Yes. Well I guess you're wondering why I would want to speak to you."

"Yes."

"As you know our Student Composition Showcase is in May. I've watched you for the past three years and I've noted your tremendous growth. Your compositions have been exceptional I want you to be one of the representatives of the junior undergraduate class and premiere one of your pieces."

"Are you serious?"

"Yes." She laughed. "Congratulations." She picked up her briefcase and walked towards the door. "Oh, by the way," she said turning around, "Make it good because everyone from the New York Philharmonic to the movie directors will be there watching. And you never know when a job opportunity might come along."

"Now unto him that is able to keep you from falling, and to present you faultless before the presence of his glory with exceeding joy, to the only wise God our Savior, be glory and majesty, dominion and power, both now and ever. Amen."

"Okay I'll see you later Naomi."

"Bye Sam."

"Are you ready to go?" Lorna nudged me.

"Hold on, I just need to speak with someone."

I walked over to Jackie. "Hi." She looked surprised to see me talk to her.

"Hi."

"I was wondering if you'd like to go out for lunch one day in the week? It would be my treat."

"You want to take me out for lunch?"

"Yeah."

She looked at me, examining if this was a joke. "Okay."

That Saturday we went to a little café in the city.

"So why did you really invite me out here?"

"I don't know, I figured we ought to get to know each other better."

"Really," She took a sip of her soda. "You haven't tried to get to know me better before."

"You never gave me a chance to."

She stayed silent and played with her food. "It's not that I don't like you, it's just..."

"I intruded on your territory."

"I guess so."

"I'm sorry you felt that way, my intention was never to step on anyone's toes."

"Don't apologize. It's my fault; I was jealous over what you had with Nathaniel. I've wanted to do this for a long time, but my pride got in the way. I'm sorry for the looks, for every word I've said, I'm sorry."

I smiled at her. "Don't worry about it, let's forget it ever happened."

"I'd like that."

Finals for my first semester classes were all this week. I had two research papers and two performances that would determine my grade. After Nathaniel and I had broken up I barely went on social media anymore. I didn't want to see pictures of him and I figured it'd be rude to block considering he'd never done anything bad to me. I could see the green circle next to his name on the side of my screen. I clicked on it and the chat window opened up.

I typed, "Hi."

I waited for a response, my heart beating erratically.

There was a long pause. I watched the talk bubble appear with those three dots.

"Hi, how are you?" he responded.

"Good. How's Haiti?"

"Good, over two hundred people have been saved and we built a school and a few homes."

"Your mom told me. That's great, how's your French coming along?"

"Good, when I get back I'll be able to follow you and Sam. How are things at school?"

"Great, I was chosen to do a showcase of my work in a concert in May. I'm so nervous thousands of people will be there."

"That's great."

He didn't write anything else and I sat there unsure of what to say.

"I miss you."

My heart was pounding again as I saw those three dots reappear.

"I miss you too."

"I'm sorry I haven't spoken to you in so long. I've been a coward."

"Well I'm no better; I could have spoken to you first."

"No, you didn't have to. It's my fault. I'm sorry for everything."

The talk bubble kept appearing and disappearing. What did I expect him to say to me?

I paused. *Should I do this?*

"There's something I have to tell you," I typed.

"What?"

I felt sick.

"You know the problems I have with my parents…"

"Yeah…"

"My stepfather used to rape me."

107

There was a long pause; I could imagine his face, disgusted.

"My mother didn't protect me. My stepfather is rich, and she wanted the finer things in life and she wasn't willing to give them up, not even for me."

"I'm so sorry; I should have never judged your situation."

"I should have told you sooner."

"I'm glad you told me now."

"I could have saved you a lot of trouble by telling you earlier."

"Naomi, don't make this your fault."

"God wants me to forgive him, but it's hard."

"It is going to be hard. I'll pray for you."

"Thank you."

I waited for a response and none came, I looked at the sidebar on my computer. The green circle was gone. His signal was gone.

It was winter break from school, I got an A on all my finals, and now I could relax. Lorna and I had just finished eating dinner and I was clearing the table.

"I spoke to Nathaniel the other day."

"You did?"

"Yeah."

"What did you talk about?"

"Just what was going on at school, in Haiti, stuff like that."

"Anything more?" she probed.

"I told him."

"Told him what?"

"About Travis and my mom."

Her head snapped up. "You did?"

"Yeah."

"That's wonderful Naomi. I'm proud of you, that took a lot of strength."

"Not my strength."

"Amen." She picked at some grapes inside a bowl. I began to wash the dishes in the sink.

"Do you think he would ever ask me again?"

"Are you speaking to me?" She said dramatically putting a hand on her chest. "Is Naomi actually speaking to me about her relationships?"

I laughed. "Yes. I am finally opening up to you about my relationships."

"You know, Naomi, I don't know." She popped a grape in her mouth. "The bigger question is whether you're ready for marriage." She looked up at me. "Are you?"

I looked down at the dish with food on it. All it took was a few good scrubbings and it would be spotless. "No," I said turning to her. "But I will be."

My phone rang. Lisa. "Hey Lisa, what's up?"

"I need to talk to you." She was crying.

"What happened?"

"Can you please come over after school?"

After school I raced to the train station. Was she hurt? Did someone die? Did she drop out of school? I frantically walked two blocks to her apartment building.

"What happened?" I said as soon as she opened the door. She walked over to the couch and sat down.

"Naomi, do you think I'm a bad person?"

I closed the door behind me. "Why would you ask me that?"

"You're not answering the question."

"I don't think any one of us is good."

"That's what I thought you'd say."

"Where is this coming from Lisa?"

"Today, when I was leaving school a girl stopped me and asked me if I thought I was a good person. So of course, I said yes. Then she started to ask me if I'd ever lied or lusted or stole something. Naomi I've done everything bad in that bible." She pointed to a bible on the couch that I had given her a couple of years ago. "All this time I thought I was good person who was going to heaven."

"There's hope. Didn't she tell you that?"

"I walked away from her, I told her I had a train to catch." I walked over to her and sat on the couch with her.

"I'm no good either, Lisa. Jesus makes me good, makes me righteousness. If you want that, all you have to do is tell him."

"I don't think he would want me anymore." *Ramona. She sounded like Ramona.*

"He loves you. All he wants is for you to return that love. Accept him, let him in Lisa."

"I don't know how."

"Let me show you how."

I couldn't sleep. I tossed and turned for hours. Lord, help me get some sleep. I turned on the TV hoping the glare would put me to sleep.

"…Sometimes we don't see eye to eye. We don't agree, we don't know why. But Jesus prayed that we'd be one. So, for the sake of God's own son"

I rose up, listening more intently. "…Shall we gather at the river of forgiveness? Come together at the waters of love, flowing like a fountain from the mercy giver. Shall we gather at the river?"

I knew what I had to do. That morning I woke up early, walking into Lorna's room.

"Lorna." I whispered, nudging her.

"Hmm?"

"Can I borrow the car? It's really important."

"Where are you going?"

"I'll tell you later, I promise. I just need the car for a few hours, I'll be back by evening."

"Okay, be safe."

"I will." I drove for an hour, my body tense and rigid. I took no stops until I reached my destination. My house. I stared at it from across the street. This house held eighteen years of nightmares for me and yet I was here. *Go back to Lorna's house.* I rested my head on the steering wheel. Two figures exited the house. My mom and Travis. He was frail; he had to have lost about 50 pounds. My mom held him up, supporting him. They got in his Mercedes and drove off not noticing me. I sat there for a while weighing my options. Go home or wait until they come back. I got out of the car and walked to the door. I lifted my hand to knock about 3 times before actually ringing the doorbell. Our housekeeper Vivian answered the door.

"Naomi!"

"Hi Viv." Vivian had started working for us when I was about 16 when my mom became tired of making her own meals.

"What are you doing here? I mean where have you been?" She gave me a huge hug. "Come in."

"How are you?" She asked when we were inside.

"I'm good."

"Oh, my goodness look how pretty you are."

I smiled, "Thank you."

"Come to the kitchen let me fix you something to eat."

I knew better than to refuse a meal when offered. "Nothing too big."

"Okay I'll promise to behave."

She fixed up an omelet. "So where have you been."

"Brooklyn."

"I hope you've been doing well."

"Yeah I go to Julliard now."

"Good for you, Naomi, you always wanted to go there." There was a long silence and I played with my food.

"How bad is he?"

"Stage three pancreatic cancer. He's not responding to medications."

"How's my mom taking it?"

"Not good, she doesn't sleep, she constantly checks to see if he's breathing during the night."

"Promise me something."

"What?"

"Promise me you won't tell them that I came here today."

"But Naomi-"

"No buts, Viv, promise me."

"I promise."

"Thank you, I'm gonna get going now."

"So soon?"

"Yeah, I have to head back."

"It was really nice seeing you again." She hugged me and held my face in her hands. "Don't stay away for too long."

"We'll see."

I left the house and drove away. *70 miles an hour.* I pressed the gas harder. *80 miles an hour.* Ten more minutes until I was out of Hewlett Bay. *You are now leaving Westchester County.* I pulled over and finally let out the scream I had been holding in.

You won't tell anyone, will you?" he said hovering over me.

"No, I won't tell."

"Because you know what will happen if you tell. You don't want to live on the dirty streets, do you?"

"No."

"So, then this is our little secret, it doesn't leave this house."

He put a finger to my lips. "Shh, don't tell anyone."

Nathaniel and I had talked online three times since our first conversation. He wasn't able to speak to me more often because of the lack of signal or the amount of work the group did that day.

"How are you?" he wrote.

"Good."

"Update me, what's going on?"

"Well, Lisa accepted Christ."

"Really, that's great! She's been coming to church?"

"Every week"

"How's Sam?"

"He's good. He's grown a lot."

"How are you?"

"I'm okay. I still haven't composed anything worth of premiering at the showcase"

"You'll come up with something."

"I hope so."

"Still too doubtful."

"Still too confident. Lol."

"I went home yesterday."

"Stop lying."

"I'm serious. I had lunch with my friend Viv. She's our housekeeper."

"Did you see your parents?"

"They were leaving when I got there. I didn't stay long enough to see them."

"Will you go back?"

"I don't know. It's hard."

"I'll pray that God gives you the strength."

"Thank you. When are you supposed to come home?"

"In June."

"Oh."

"I wish I could be there to see your showcase."

"Me too."

"Miss. Beckford have you finished a piece yet?"

"No, Mrs. Reiser but I will. I have other pieces; it's just that I'm looking for the right one."

"I hope you find the right one soon."

"I will."

"Grab from life experiences, fuse things together that happened in the past and things present or things to come."

Things in the past and things present. Why hadn't I thought of that? "Thank you, Mrs. Reiser," I said racing towards the door.

"I'm sorry, are you in a hurry to go somewhere?"

I smiled. "Yes, I have to go write a masterpiece."

"I'm definitely looking forward to hearing that." She said as I walked out the door. I impatiently tapped on the glass in the train the entire way home. I raced the entire way home, my feet tingling when I finally got to the house. I ran up the stairs.

"Whoa, what's the hurry?" Lorna said.

"I've got to get some staff paper."

"New piece."

"No, Lorna THE piece."

"Well I'll leave you to your work."

I sat down on my bed grabbing my violin out of its case. I took a deep breath. *Think the past.* Cold hands, secrets, betrayal, and pain. I turned on the recorder on the computer playing my violin. *The present.* God, joy, peace, family and love. And the future? *What did the future hold?* Forgiveness and Healing.

I started working at 6:00 in the evening and by 2:00 in the morning; it was finished.

"Wake up, Naomi." Lorna was nudging me.
"Hmm."
"Time to go to school."
I groaned.
"You stayed up all night, didn't you?"
"Yeah."
"Well, no pain no gain. Come on, up, up, up!"
I sat up looking at her. "I did it, it's perfect."
"Don't tell me what it's like I want to be surprised."
"You will be."
I showered, dressed, and grabbed a croissant as I headed out the door. I took my cell phone out of my pocket.
"Hello."
"Hey, Lisa, I know it's a little late, but I was wondering if you'd help me pick out a dress for the showcase."
"I thought you'd never ask."
"So, when can we go shopping."
"Shopping won't be necessary."
"What do you mean?"
"I started to make you a dress."
"Seriously?"
"Naomi, it's gorgeous, it's yellow and it'll really enhance your complexion and your figure. I just need you to come so I can make some adjustments to it, so it can fit you perfectly."

"Lisa, you're the best, you know that?"

"Yeah I know. Come over today after school."

"Okay, I'll see you later."

I was finally able to give Mrs. Reiser the good news and get together with a harpist. After my first class I practiced for an hour.

"Okay, we'll take an hour lunch." I made my way to the cafeteria. I grabbed my phone and messaged Nathaniel.

"Hey."

"Hey, shouldn't you be at school?" he asked.

"I'm at lunch."

"So…."

"So, I finished my piece."

"I knew you would. I hope I get to hear it when I get back."

"You know everything. Yeah, I guess I could play it for you."

"I'm looking forward to it."

"I hope you like it."

"I know I'll love it."

"So……."

"So, I'll see you soon."

"Yeah two months from now."

"Time flies, I'll be there sooner than you think."

My phone vibrated. Incoming call. Westchester County.

I answered the call.

"Hello?"

"Hello, Naomi, it's Viv."

"Hey, is everything ok?"

"Sorry I know this is weird. I found your number in your mom's files. She tracked you."

"Yeah, she's always been good at stuff like that."

"Mr. Travis is in the hospital. The doctors say he only has a few weeks."

I sucked in a deep breath. "A few weeks?"

"Yes, he's now having trouble keeping down food." I rested my head in my hand. "Which hospital?"

"NYU Medical Center."

"Okay. Thanks for telling me Viv."

I hung up. What was I going to do? I didn't want to see him. I don't even know if I'll be able to even carry a conversation with him. *My grace is sufficient.*

"I need more than grace right now." I whispered.

My strength is made perfect in your weakness.

"Hey Sam." I said as I walked in to the backroom of the Riviera.

"Hey."

"I brought your ticket. Remember to wear a nice suit or something."

"You know I hate getting dressed up."

"You can do it this one time. Just for me."

"Just for you. Thanks for the ticket, kid."

"Kid? Sam, I'm twenty-three years old. Don't you think I've outgrown that nickname now?"

"You'll always be 'kid' to me."

"Yeah, well I guess I can live with that."

"So, I'll see you on Friday."

"Yeah, see you on Friday."

"I'm proud of you."

"Thanks Sam." I left the Riviera and took the train to Lisa's apartment.

"Hey, I got your ticket."

"Come on, let's get you into that dress, I want to make sure it fits you like a glove."

"Okay let me see it."

"Oh no, you can't see it yet." She held up a blindfold.

"Are you serious?"

"Very. Turn around." I turned around and she tied the blindfold around my eyes.

She helped me into the dress and I felt the zipper go up. "Okay. Can I see now?"

"Hold on just a moment. Lift your hair." I felt her put a necklace on me. "Okay, you may look at yourself." She took the blindfold off. I looked beautiful. I couldn't speak.

"That's exactly the reaction I was hoping for."

"Lisa, this is beautiful."

"No, you're beautiful. You make the dress."

"Thank you." I said hugging her.

"You're very welcome." She reached into her closet pulling out a green, one shoulder ball gown. "You know I couldn't leave myself out of this."

"You made this too?"

"Um hm."

"It's gorgeous."

She turned me towards the mirror. "Friday is your night. You are the belle of the ball. You will do perfect and you will get a job that pays a gazillion dollars." We both laughed. "All you need is prince charming," she said, sitting on her bed.

"He's in Haiti. And what makes you think he's even interested in me like that anymore? I haven't seen him in two years."

"Absence makes the heart grow fonder."

"I turned him down once, why would he even want to have a relationship with me again?"

"Come on look at you. You're pretty, you're smart, and you love God. What more could he ask for? The real question is, if he asked you again would you say yes?"

I looked at her, thinking. "Yes. I would say yes."

"So, tomorrow's the big day." Lorna said coming into my room.

"Yeah. I'm nervous and excited at the same time."

"You know when I first saw you, you reminded me so much of myself. For a few moments it was like I was living on the streets again. You've lived here for four years and I've watched you grow so much. I remember the girl who hated Christ, who hated life. And now I stand before the woman who has eternal life. The Lord has indeed blessed me by sending you into my life."

"No, I think he sent you into mine."

"I'm so proud of you."

"Lorna, I have something to tell you."

"Remember when I took the car last month and I was gone all day?"

"Yes."

"I went to Hewlett Bay, to my house. I went to see them, but I chickened out, so I waited until they left, and I saw my friend Viv, she's our housekeeper. He's really sick, he has cancer. Right now, he's at NYU Medical."

"So, what are you going to do?"

"I don't know."

"I know you'll do the right thing."

"I don't have to see him to forgive him, do I?"

"Only you know that."

Today was a whirlwind of events. I woke up at 9:00 in the morning and took a long shower. I polished my violin and Lorna sent me off to the hair dresser. When I got back home Lisa came over in the afternoon and did my makeup and helped me into my dress.

"Come on girls, its 5:00!" Lorna called from downstairs.

"Okay, let's go."

"Oh no, you can't just walk downstairs like that. You have to be announced."

"You are such a drama queen."

"Just let me do my thing."

"Okay, go do your thing."

I heard her go down stairs. "And now presenting Miss. Naomi Beckford."

I walked downstairs. "Oh, Naomi you look like a princess." Lorna said, while taking pictures.

"I told you. You're the belle of the ball."

"Alright, we have to go. I don't have much time."

The entire way to the concert we sang songs and told jokes. When I got there, I went backstage. Every representative from every musical category was there. I looked over my music about five times making sure I remembered every note.

"Hello everyone," Mrs. Reiser and a few other teachers silenced everyone. "The show starts in five minutes, so I just want to give you a word of encouragement. I know you are nervous but let this night count. Do you best, pour your heart out, make your music speak. I wish you the very best tonight."

Breathe. Just breathe. I sat down on a chair and rubbed my hands together. *Lord, help me be a blessing. Give me the strength.*

"Good night and welcome to the Julliard School of Music Student Composition Showcase. We have selected twenty-four exceptional students to showcase their original compositions for you. We hope that you enjoy the pieces and most of all recognize the tremendous talent that lies within all of our students."

She called the first performer, a piano major. I was number fourteen on the program. Time seemed to move in slow motion. I didn't even leave the backroom at the intermission. I was two people away. I watched the guitarist and the saxophone player before me. My hands shook as I held my violin.

"Next, we have Naomi Beckford, a violin major. She's here to play her sonata entitled The Road to Forgiveness."

I walked out on stage the lights blinding me. I couldn't see any faces. My hands and knees shook. *Lord help me.* I played the first note. I closed my eyes. Scenes flashed before my eyes. Travis' first day at the house. My senses opened. The cold of the bathroom floor. The look on my mother's face. The faint beeping of a heart monitor. The loneliness of the shelter. The joy of finding Christ. The first time he told me he loved me. His pain when I said no. The pain of losing him. The peace Christ had given me. *How much had passed since I started?* I couldn't remember. I was about to open my eyes until something else washed over me. I didn't know what to call it. Grace, Mercy, Forgiveness.

My grace is sufficient. I finally understood. He had carried me through these two years. I remember reading, Proverbs 3:5-6, "Trust in the LORD with all thine heart; and lean not unto thine own understanding. In all thy ways acknowledge him, and he shall direct thy paths."

"Thank you, Lord." I mouthed as I played my last note.

I looked out into the crowd smiling, knowing that even though I couldn't see them that they could see me. I drank tons of water after I performed, wetting my dry throat. After the show every performer took a bow and I went backstage and a security guard approached me.

"Naomi Beckford?"

"Yes."

"Stay behind, a fan is here to see you."

"A fan?"

"Hey, I guess you're famous already."

I wondered if it was the leader of the New York Philharmonic or Steven Spielberg. I walked out on to the stage and waited. The theater was completely empty by now. I saw the door in the back open. A masculine figure walked through the door holding something; I couldn't see it was too far away. I put my hand over my eyes, shielding the stage lights. The figure walked closer. I still couldn't see. I walked to the edge of the stage. My breath caught. Nathaniel. He continued walking stopping a few feet from me. He held a bouquet of roses in his hand. He looked the same, but different somehow. He looked stronger, wiser.

"I believe these are for you." he handed me the roses. "Bravo, you were magnificent tonight."

"What are you doing here?"

"I took an early leave, I couldn't miss this."

I couldn't breathe, couldn't think. "I can't believe you're here. Everyone was in on this weren't they?"

"They may have had something to do with it."

"This is amazing, like an answer to a prayer."

He walked onto the stage. "You know on the plane ride here I read Genesis."

"You did?"

"Yeah I love Genesis; I often put myself in the stories. Want to know my favorite one?"

"Do tell."

"When Jacob stole his brother's birthright, he fled to his uncle Laban's house. And when he got there the first person he saw was Rachel. And when he saw her he kissed her and wept. Now Jacob loved Rachel and he said to Laban, 'I will serve thee seven years for Rachel thy younger daughter.' And Laban agreed, and Jacob worked seven years for Rachel, but they seemed but a few days to him because of the love he had for her."

I smiled. "Well it hasn't exactly been seven years."

He laughed, and I saw his dimples. "No, it hasn't." He took my hand in his. "I'm willing to wait for you, even if it takes seven more years for you to marry me, I'll wait."

I looked at him and put my hand to his cheek. "I don't think seven years will be necessary." He looked at me and smiled wide. Suddenly he picked me up and twirled me around as we both laughed. He put me down and reached into his pocket. He pulled out a little black box and opened it.

"Marry me?"

"Yes." He slid the ring on my finger, kissed me and wiped my tears.

"I love you." I said taking his hand. "Will you do something for me?"

"Anything."

"I need you to take me somewhere."

We pulled up to NYU Medical Center. "What's going on Naomi?"

"My stepfather is here. He's sick, I have to see him."

He looked at me nodding his head in understanding. We walked to the nurses' station.

"Hello, may I please see a Mr. Travis Cohen."

"Miss, it's after visiting hours and you are in ICU, you have to be relative of the patient."

"He's my stepfather."

"You'll have to come tomorrow."

"Please, I don't know if this is my last chance to see him. I am asking you for a favor, please."

She looked at me weighing her options. "You can go, but I'm sorry sir I can't let you in, I don't want to be held liable."

"Thanks fine." Nathaniel said.

She gave me a pass. "Room 311. If anyone asks you questions just show them this and tell them Mary sent you up there."

"Thank you so much."

Nathaniel took my hand. "You'll be alright?"

"Yeah. I'll be alright."

He kissed me forehead before letting go of my hand. I walked down the hall and took the elevator to the third floor. I walked down the hall trying to seem natural in the hospital, I could see everyone looking at me wondering why I was here in a ball gown. But no one stopped me. No one asked for any ID. I stopped at the door. *Room 311*. I sucked in a deep breath and knocked.

"Come in."

I opened the door and walked in. My mother froze. Travis seeing my mother's expression turned his head towards me. *Shock.* That's the only word I could use to describe their faces.

"Naomi." my mother whispered.

"Yes, it's me."

"I didn't think you would come."

"I didn't think I would come either."

She rose up from her chair and walked slowly over to me. "How are you?"

"Good. I just came from a performance for my school."

"Julliard, right?"

"Yes."

She looked at me for a long time, taking in every new feature.

"What made you come?"

I looked over at Travis. "I have to talk to you."

He didn't say a word, he simply looked at me. He was so thin I could see every vein in his hand. He had tubes all over him and I can see him laboriously breathing.

"I always thought you were the one that ruined my life. I blamed you for everything, when I failed, when I came short or missed the mark." My eyes were misting. "You took something from me, something that I can never buy back. You forever changed my life at the age of eight. I was a child." My chin trembled, and I fought to keep my emotions under control. "How could you do that to me? I always tried to figure it out. I hated you because of what you stole from me." I turned to my mother. "And I hated you because you didn't protect me."

I walked closer to him now. "I have spent fifteen years living with bitterness and anger in my heart and I don't want to do it anymore." My voice broke. "With every ounce of strength, I have within me, and even the strength I don't have, I forgive you. From the depths of my soul I forgive you. May God have mercy on your soul, just as he has had mercy on mine."

I could hear my mother silently crying. His eyes were pooling with water. "I'm sorry," he said silently. "I'm so sorry."

I took a seat next to him and held his hands in mine. They were cold.

"He loves you, no matter what you've done, he loves you. God demonstrates his own love for us in this, while we were yet sinners. Christ died for us."

"I pray that he will forgive someone like me, I don't deserve to see him in eternity." his voice strained.

"I tell you the truth; today you will meet him in paradise."

He bawled in my arms and I spent the night warming his cold hands in mine and by morning he was gone. I didn't feel the gloating of vengeance. I felt peace that my soul was now free.

Grace found me.

Thank you so much for reading Grace Found Me. It was such a blessing to revisit this book 10 years later. It reminded so much of where God has brought me spiritually and in my writing career. I want you all to be excited about my next novel, *When Seeds Fall,* a historical romance about Black Wall Street and Rosewood, FL. I'm overjoyed to share this excerpt with you.

"Wake up!" I felt someone jostling me awake. "Wake up!" I opened my eyes and looked up at Charles.

"Hmmm?" I mumbled.

"Which one are you?"

"What?" I said sitting up and wiping my eyes.

"What's your name?" He said, putting a hand on my shoulder.

"Marcie!" I said, slapping his hand away. I looked around, suddenly feeling alarmed. "Where's Margie?"

He stood stone faced. "Looks like your sister left us a present," he said handing me a folded piece of paper.

I rushed to open it.

Marcie, I know you wanted to go West, but I really think it's best for me to go north to New York. I know you'll be angry with me, but maybe it's a good thing for us to split up, to finally know what it's like to be our own person. I've been thinking maybe it will be good for you to go west with Mr. Sanderson. At least in Tulsa you will know someone, rather than going all the way to California by yourself. I bought you and Mr. Sanderson a ticket to Tulsa. I hope that will help you forgive me for taking the rest for a ticket to New York. Oh, please tell Charles that it wasn't anything personal and that I only took his wallet because I needed his address. I hope to write once I reach New York to let you know I am safe. I love you Marcie, even if you hate me right now, and I wish you a life of adventure.

Margie.

I couldn't move. I felt like I'd swallowed a rock. I tried to catch my breath and felt my hand shaking.

"Marcie?"

She's never been on her own, she could get hurt, she could get raped.

"Marcie."

How does she even know John will take her in? She'll be a woman of ill repute living with a man she's not married to.

"Marcie!"

I snapped out of my trance. "I have to go after her," I said getting up.

"Oh, trust me I would if I could," he said, with a scowl on his face. "But, it seems the train to New York has left and our train leaves in half hour."

"Who cares? She's my sister!"

"And a thief!"

He was breathing just as hard as I was. He stepped back and rubbed his forehead. "Look, she left me with nothing else except this ticket back home, so there is no option of going after her, although I'd do it just for the satisfaction."

His eyes were tired, and his tie was loosened around his neck. "Did she take everything from you too?"

I nodded. "Except for a ticket for Tulsa. Says we should go together so I won't be alone."

His eyes widened. "Let me see that letter," he said, snatching it out of my hands.

I watched him read before he burst out in anger. "It wasn't personal?!"

"Mr. Sanderson."

He paced. "She steals money from me, and it's not personal?"

"Mr. Sanderson!"

He stopped. "I'm sorry. I'm just-"

"Angry?"

He sighed. "Yes. Angry is an accurate word."

"I understand," I said, biting my lip. "I'm very sorry." I felt the heat in my face and the sting of coming tears. "For all of this."

"It's not your fault," he said, sitting next to me.

"Yes it is! I was always letting her influence me and have her own way! Now look at this!"

"Makes no sense to blame yourself. She's made her own choices. Like she said, she wants you to live separately from her."

I shook my head. "I don't know how."

"Well, it's never too late to learn." He got up and held out his hand. "Come on. We've got a train to catch."

I shook my head in astonishment. "You'd still want me to go to Tulsa with you?"

He shrugged. "Yeah, why not? I'll need a traveling companion," he said winking. I smiled in spite of myself. He picked up my bag and nudged his head forward. I got up and started to walk alongside him. "Oh, by the way, on this train you'll go by Mrs. Sanderson. Wouldn't want anyone thinking the worst of you."

I looked out the window at the Louisiana scenery passing by. Adventure.... Well, at least Margie was getting her wish. I certainly was embarking on an adventure, leaving the only place I'd ever known and heading to Tulsa with a perfect stranger.

Mr. Sanderson, tugged his pants free of the ripped leather of our seats. "Don't you just love Jim Crow?" he said, his tone drawling.

"No way to escape it," I said absentmindedly.

"Well, I think you'll like Greenwood. Self-sufficient black community."

I turned from the window to meet his eyes. "*The* Greenwood?"

"Yes, *the* Greenwood."

"As in the *Negro Wall Street* Greenwood?" I asked excitedly.

"Yes."

I sighed, a smile on my lips. "I take it you've heard about it," he said.

"Yes, I've been reading about it for years," I said. "I thought Margie would've really liked to go, with all the successful people there and all."

"Yes, I'm sure Margie would've been on the prowl in Greenwood."

I smacked his arm. "Don't talk about my sister that way!"

ABOUT THE AUTHOR

Shaida Escoffery is the author of several books including Idle, Wild, Love and Bloom. Born in Brooklyn, NY and raised in Miami, FL, she is the alumna of both the University of Miami and New York University's Graduate School.

www.ingramcontent.com/pod-product-compliance
Lightning Source LLC
Chambersburg PA
CBHW021111130626
46554CB00002B/645